the
woman
who
didn't
grow
old

Grégoire Delacourt is the bestselling author of nine novels and has won several literary awards. His novel *The List of My Desires* was a runaway number-one international bestseller. Grégoire lives with his wife in Brooklyn, New York.

Vineet Lal studied French at the University of Edinburgh and Princeton University. He has translated many successful French authors, including Guillaume Musso.

Also available from W&N

The List of My Desires
The First Thing You See
We Only Saw Happiness

the woman who didn't grow old

Grégoire Delacourt

Translated from the French
by Vineet Lal

First published in Great Britain in 2020 by Weidenfeld & Nicolson
This paperback edition published in 2021 by Weidenfeld & Nicolson
an imprint of The Orion Publishing Group Ltd
Carmelite House, 50 Victoria Embankment
London EC4Y 0DZ

An Hachette UK Company

1 3 5 7 9 10 8 6 4 2

A CIP catalogue record for this book
is available from the British Library.

ISBN (Paperback) 978 1 4746 1 219 7
ISBN (eBook) 978 1 4746 1220 3

Typeset by Input Data Services Ltd, Somerset

Printed and bound in Great Britain by Clays Ltd, Elcograf S.p.A.

www.weidenfeldandnicolson.co.uk
www.orionbooks.co.uk

For my mother,
who hasn't aged for a very long time,
and was especially fond of the number seven.

One to Thirty-Five

I

When I was a year old, I was a perfect match for my age.

A charming little twig, seventy-four centimetres tall, blessed with an ideal weight of 9.3 kilos, a head circumference of forty-six centimetres, sprouting a mop of blonde curls and a woolly hat on days when it was windy.

After being breastfed, I had turned to drinking more than half a litre of milk a day, and I was given a few vegetables, carbohydrates and proteins to enrich my diet. At teatime I'd have home-made compote and, every so often, a few morsels of food that melted under my palate, like sorbet.

At the age of one, I also took my first steps – there's a photo to prove it. While I was skipping around like an awkward little deer, occasionally tripping over a rug or a coffee table, Colette and Matisse took their final bow, Simone de Beauvoir won the Goncourt prize and Jane Campion came into the world little knowing that, thirty-nine years later, she would move me to tears by placing a grand piano on a New Zealand beach.

At two, my growth curve filled my parents and paediatrician with pride.

When I was three, four second molars were added to the collection of teeth in my mouth, which already included eight incisors, four first molars and four canines. But Maman still preferred to grind the walnuts and almonds I insisted on having, for fear that I might choke.

I was almost a metre in height, ninety-six centimetres to be precise, and my weight was statistically noteworthy: fourteen kilos, perfect for my age, distributed with a great deal of finesse. The circumference of my head came to fifty-two centimetres, going by my health record book, and Papa's time in Algeria was extended. He would send us letters filled with sadness, photos of himself surrounded by his friends – they'd be smoking, sometimes laughing, sometimes they seemed depressed. They were maybe twenty-two, twenty-five, twenty-six; they looked like children dressed as grown-ups.

You had the feeling they wouldn't grow any older.

At five, I was just like any girl of five ought to be. I ran,

4

I jumped, I pedalled, I climbed, I danced. I was good with my hands, I could draw well, I would argue, I was curious about everything, I refused to say rude words. I would dress up as a seven-year-old and feel rather proud of myself; then there was an uprising in Algiers and Papa came home.

He had a leg missing and I didn't recognise him.

At six and a half, I began losing my incisors and my expression would see-saw between a grimace and an idiotic grin. I managed to skip the metallic taste in my mouth, the tooth fairy and the one-franc coins under my pillow.

At eight, records show that I was 124 centimetres tall and weighed twenty kilos. I wore cotton jersey shirts, gingham skirts, a little bib-fronted dress and, for my Sunday best, a silk taffeta frock. Ribbons fluttered in my hair, like butterflies. Maman loved taking pictures of me. She used to say that beauty doesn't last – it always flies away, like a bird from a cage. It's important to fix it in our memory; important to thank it for having chosen us.

Maman was my princess.

At eight, I was aware of my sexuality.

I knew the difference between sadness and disappointment, pride and joy, anger and jealousy. I knew I was upset because Papa still wasn't brave enough to let me sit on his knees, despite his new prosthetic leg. I knew about joy, when he was in good spirits; then we would play together, he would pretend to be Long John Silver, thrilling me with tales of wonder, of buried treasure and the high seas. I knew disappointment, when he was in pain, when he'd be in a foul mood and turn into a different Long John Silver, a bad-tempered and menacing one.

At nine, I learnt at school how people managed to move around, and lit their streets and homes, on the eve of the French Revolution. We were told about Gambetta's escape in a hot-air balloon, while above our heads a Russian had been orbiting in space – he would later give his name to a crater that measured 265 kilometres in diameter.

At ten, I bore a shocking resemblance to a little girl of ten. I dreamt of having a fringe on my forehead like Jane Banks in *Mary Poppins*, which we'd gone to see as a family at the cinema, Le Royal. I dreamt of having a brother or sister too, but Papa didn't want any more children in a world that saw fit to kill them.

He never talked to us about Algeria.

He had found work as a glazier – a balancing act on a stepladder, he would chuckle, and a one-legged guy won't be running the show! He often fell, or cursed his absent leg, and each new step he climbed was a victory: I'm doing this for your mother, so she can see I'm no cripple. He liked to look around people's homes. To study others closely. He was reassured to see that suffering was everywhere. That young men of his age had returned from Algeria with wounds that would never heal, their hearts ripped out, lips sewn together to avoid the unspeakable, eyelids glued shut to avoid reliving the horrors.

He glazed over the silence as if closing up a scar.

Maman was beautiful.

Sometimes she came home with flushed cheeks. Then Long John Silver would smash a plate or a glass before tearfully apologising for being so clumsy and picking up the shattered fragments of his sorrow.

At ten, I was 138.3 centimetres tall, I weighed 32.5 kilos

and my body surface area was close to one square metre – a micron, in terms of the universe. I was graceful, I would sing 'Da Doo Ron Ron' and 'Be-Bop-A-Lula' in our yellow kitchen to make everyone laugh, and one evening Papa made me sit on his sole remaining leg.

At twelve, I noticed my areolae getting larger and darker; I could feel two buds starting to open under my chest.

Maman had taken to wearing skirts that left her knees bare, thanks to a certain Mary Quant, in England; it wasn't long before they revealed almost all of her thighs. She had long, pale legs and I prayed that one day I'd have the same.

On some evenings she never came home at all, but Papa didn't break any more plates or glasses.

His work was going well. He no longer only repaired frames or replaced panes damaged by storms or vandalism, but also installed windows in the modern houses that were shooting up everywhere around the town, attracting new families, cars and roundabouts – and a few unsavoury types as well.

He was keen that we leave our apartment so that we, too, could move into one of the pristine new homes. They've got gardens and huge bathrooms, he would say, and fully-fitted kitchens. Your mother would be happy. That was all he really hoped for. In the meantime, he had bought a television set, a Grandin Caprice, and we would sit there in fascination, watching *Playing with Words* and *Starring Your Favourite Songs*, without talking about her, without expecting her back, without joy.

Then I turned thirteen.

At the beginning of the summer, Maman went to Le

Royal with a friend to see a film by a young director who was only twenty-eight: *A Man and a Woman*. When she came out of the cinema she was laughing and singing, and as she danced on the road an ochre Ford Taunus took her from us.

She had just turned thirty-five.

I'd always thought she was immortal.

At thirteen, I suddenly grew old.

2

I felt a shiver of cold.

The room was poorly lit and Maman was lying on a bed that looked hard; her long legs and body were draped in a white sheet. Her beautiful features were still intact and yet her beauty had already flown away. I later found out how the undertakers managed to preserve the image of serenity and the illusion of life: injections with a hypodermic needle, to restore the face's natural appearance, filling up the sagging flesh around the earlobes, cheeks and chin. This process also allowed them to reinstate the plumpness of the deceased, in cases where they might have lost a lot of weight during the time preceding their death.

Which wasn't the case with Maman. She had simply been torn away. Torn apart.

Papa was crying; I wrapped my arms around his big, lopsided pirate body. We comforted each other in the silence.

I didn't cry because Maman used to say that tears would spoil your face.

Later, he took off his coat and used it to cover Maman's body; she'll catch cold here, he said, but he was the one who caught a cold that day.

His heart turned to stone.

I didn't dare talk to Maman aloud, not in that ghastly room – a bouquet of plastic flowers in a dark corner, without fragrance or dew, a book for noting the cries of anguish she would never read, the juddering rattle of the air conditioning.

I let the words clatter around my chest, choke in my throat and escape between my lips in a muffled haze. Then I took my leave, as if bidding farewell before going back to war, and returned to the street, to the blare of murderous cars, the mildness of spring, the faint scent of summer that already hung in the air; and suddenly Papa was beside me, towering, an oak tree.

At the local café, he asked for an extra-large glass of beer that he downed in one and I had a mint cordial. Then he ordered a kir that he left on the table – she used to love kir – and, as the mixture of alcohol and grief began to take hold, he broke down: it's not because she's no longer here that she's no longer here.

At thirteen, I understood what it means to be alone.

Later, the family arrived. Maman's brother, who lived in Talloires and prepped rally cars. He was accompanied by someone who wasn't his wife; she looked like Françoise Hardy, the woman who sang 'The House Where I Grew Up' – the latest hit that Maman and I would belt out, screaming hysterically, into wooden spoons that served as mikes. Papa's parents also came, from Valenciennes, their skin as grey as the sky in Nord, their eyes as dark as schist, bound inseparably to each other – two barnacles on a rock. They were concerned about their son: won't be easy, meetin' someone, not when you've a kid 'n' a peg leg, that's for sure. For sure, nodded the other.

And that was all.

Our family was a species on the verge of extinction. A flower that would no longer open in the morning.

There was a wake at the house when we returned from the graveyard, and some of Maman's friends had brought *gâteaux*, and memories, because you really need to remember the good times if you want to keep going until the end. To stay alive.

Marion, with whom Maman had gone to see the Claude Lelouch film, gave me a photo of her. It was a colour instant photo, taken with one of those new Polaroid cameras. Maman in front of Le Royal. Maman smiling at the lens. Maman with a ginger fringe and a Cardin dress. Maman, two hours before the Ford Taunus. Maman, looking beautiful. So beautiful. Immortally beautiful.

At thirteen, I discovered that beauty does not last.

3

At fifteen, thank God, my adolescent hormones had no effect on my mood, my state of mind or my behaviour.

I was therefore neither aggressive, nor rebellious, nor overexcited, nor ill at ease with myself, nor even hyper-sensitive or tearful – although I confess I still cried my eyes out at the end of *The Graduate* when Dustin Hoffman yells 'Elaine! Elaine! Elaine!', but that was for different reasons.

By fifteen, I had turned into a delightful young girl, despite the cruel absence of Maman. Without her advice on what to wear, putting on make-up, trying out waxing for the first time, knowing what to say and not to say to men as old as Papa, thirsty men who wanted to share a lemonade with me. Or to boys of my own age – over-eager, charming and gawky – who fantasised about the unknown, about luck and mostly about breasts, and who showed off by mumbling their way through the latest Bob Dylan, 'I'll Be Your Baby Tonight'.

Maman hadn't had the chance to teach me about men and their hunger, or women and their sighs.

At fifteen, my heart was broken for the first time.

I wrote a farewell letter to my torturer and another to the whole world who, clearly, didn't understand a thing.

I stole one of Papa's razor blades, wrapped in waxed paper; but the moment I picked it up, I nicked the tip of my right thumb and a drop of blood bubbled out. I was petrified – and everything returned to normal.

I missed Maman, I missed her arms and her breath. I was the orphaned child of every pore in her being, every hair, every syllable she'd not had time to share with me – like Papa, I was now walking on just one leg.

Papa's leg, however, led him to Françoise, forty years old, divorced, with a son of my age, Michel. Françoise was a pleasant sales assistant at Le Chat Noir, a shoe shop near what used to be the indoor market, who was distraught that Papa was always forced to buy a pair of shoes even though he only wore the left one. Her distress managed to crack the stone in his heart, allowing a few promises, a warm breeze and other sweet nothings to pour inside, and

Papa, if you'll pardon the expression, jumped feet first into her open arms.

At sixteen, I carried on growing.

I was then one metre sixty-five, I weighed fifty-two kilos – trousers hung on me like they did on Twiggy, according to the saleswoman at Nouvelles Galeries – and I'd gone for a change of hairstyle, a bouffant ponytail. In Paris, cobbles flew left and right, it was forbidden to forbid anything, people shouted about making love, not war, and I was certainly up for that. Oh yes: an attractive boy a little older than me had even suggested it, after he'd kissed me a few times and fondled me rather boldly, but I hadn't yet dared give away what I could only give away once.

That year, because of the widespread chaos, candidates for the *baccalauréat* only had to sit oral exams and the great majority of final-year pupils had passed by the start of the summer.

In September, Papa married Françoise. Michel became my half-brother. Everything about him was dark. He would look at me without seeing me. We were never friends. Just acquaintances.

We finally moved into the suburbs, into one of those new houses with a garden, a huge bathroom, fully-fitted kitchen and gas fireplace that could, so Papa said, have made Maman happy. But that was before that trip to the cinema. Before Anouk Aimée. Before Jean-Louis Trintignant. Before the beach, the white Ford Mustang and the music of Francis Lai.

At almost seventeen, I fell in love with Steve McQueen, after seeing *Bullitt* at Le Royal, and Jean-Marc Delahaye, after hearing him play 'Mammy Blue' on the guitar.

I found it easier to give myself to the second one.

It happened at his place, in the tiny bed in his tiny boy's bedroom, with Castrol, MV Agusta and Yamaha stickers plastered across the door, and posters of the road racer Giacomo Agostini pinned to the ceiling. It was all madly romantic. Jean-Marc was considerate enough to pull out in time, with a smile on his face, but when he began putting words to what we'd just experienced, I hurriedly got dressed again and fled.

In the street I laughed and sang, I danced, a car raced past and blew its horn as it brushed against me, and I knew, Maman, that you were by my side that day, that you were dancing with me. That I had finally become your friend.

I returned home with flushed cheeks, but Long John Silver didn't break anything.

He simply said you look out of breath, Martine (God, how I hated my name), and I began to sob. I told him that I missed Maman, that it still hurt as much as ever. He got up, poured a little crème de cassis into a glass, then filled it with white wine and placed it on the table. He said I'm sorry, I'm doing the best I can, Martine; he said I know you only ever have one *maman* and, for an instant, she was there with us.

Then Françoise and Michel came home in turn. We laid the table, I heated the gratin and made a salad. Words flew here and there, in a flurry of chirping and squawking – Françoise was telling us about her day at Le Chat Noir, Papa was smiling as he listened; Michel was raving about the Mobymatic he dreamt of owning, with its Dimoby double-clutch and variator, it could do almost fifty-three kilometres an hour, can you imagine, Henry? – Henry, that's Papa – and Papa listened indulgently while looking at me on the sly. For the first time, I could tell from his eyes that he loved me with all his heart.

Michel and I always kept as far apart as possible – not out of malice, purely indifference.

As for Françoise, she always had the good grace to hold Papa's right arm, to walk on the side where his leg had been blown off by a field gun, near Palestro in Kabylie. She was his crutch. His wing.

Papa loved her – but with a love quite different to the fire that had consumed him with Maman, or so it seems in hindsight.

With Maman, love had been a forge, the clang of iron, blind rage and flying sparks, searing burns and soothing balm. It had been passion, carnal and unrestrained, until the gunfire in Algeria – his body surrendered, stripped bare of elation and song. Orgasm had given way to silence. Impotence was gnawing at him from within. And when Maman came home in the evenings with flushed cheeks, not because she'd cheated on a disabled man but because she'd managed to ease her sorrow, it was his missing leg that poked at the smouldering coals. Then he would try to dampen the embers with alcohol, but this only inflamed his wounds even more. I think he shouted and screamed because he was afraid. He broke things because his body was broken. Because his heart was in pieces.

At seventeen, I finally saw my father smile again.

4

Then Lille.

The Catholic University, the 'Catho', the first year of an arts degree, in the striking building on Boulevard Vauban.

I was about to turn eighteen, I wore skirts that sometimes flew up in the air, revealing my long, pale legs – thank you, Maman – and I was studying eighteenth-century theatre, Goldoni, Favart, Marivaux, the semiology of the image and Latin.

In the evenings we used to meet up, around twenty students in all, at the newly opened Pubstore, with its bizarre copper façade, pierced with portholes. That was where I drank my first cocktails, smoked my first cigarettes, and a little marijuana, and where I stumbled across a few idealists who dreamt of redefining the world and the borders of the human soul. Two of them drifted into my arms and nestled against my heart, but never within it. And then there was Christian, with his dazzling charm and crystal-clear eyes. Christian for whom – despite the outfits I chose just for him, my eyelids smeared in make-up to please him in dusky shades of purple, green or blue, like the colours of twilight, despite my glossy lips simply calling out to be kissed, despite my skin that said yes – I remained invisible. The savage wound of indifference.

Back then, I would stagger my way through the days and nights. Life seemed endless and its vastness was exhilarating. We discovered independent American cinema at Le Kino, we would talk about Vietnam until daybreak, or listen to Joan Baez, and Neil Young's 'Ohio', over and over again. Each of us saw ourselves changing the world, making certain words vanish from it completely, such as *misery*, *hunger* and *injustice*. But misery, hunger and injustice were far away, on the other side of the earth, beyond the seas – a sort of true-life opera that slipped through our fingers.

I used to go home on weekends. In the train, I would escape from my academic life and turn back into a hopeless young girl of almost eighteen. In film magazines I would gaze at the eternal youth of Liz Taylor, Ursula Andress and Raquel Welch, captured in photographs that froze their beauty for ever, not the slightest trace of a wrinkle, not even a hint of fear. It felt like the stuff of dreams, because no one likes things that decay with time – they give us the feeling they're dying.

Maman's beauty would never fade.

At home, I would spend time with Françoise and Papa – he was delighted with his new articulated prosthesis, even if he needed his hands to bend it – and whiled away lazy hours dulled by sleepy small-town thinking. One evening, we'd been talking about the recent manifesto by 343 women in favour of abortion and Françoise, somewhat amused, had shrugged, assuring us that wouldn't happen, they'd never allow babies to be murdered, and I'd said nothing. I didn't tell her about the winds of change, about the wind billowing up behind women, like sails, because there's frankly no point in trying to be right.

In those days, Michel and his terrifying little gang used to ride around on their Mobymatic Chaudrons, tearing along the local roads at fifty-three kilometres an hour. They would invite themselves to dances and weddings, often getting into fights or flying off in a rage. My half-brother had chosen darkness and left his mother in tears. I had lost a *maman*, she was losing a child.

Then along came my eighteenth birthday, and with it came André.

5

I was eighteen. I really did look the part: the fragrance of freshly cut grass, one metre seventy – my adult height – and fifty-two kilos. *Tut-tut*, a bit skinny, Martine, said Long John Silver, here, have some more pasta, it's delicious. I had short hair à la Jean Seberg in *Saint Joan*, which gave me a gamine look, a modern slant I simply adored. I had perfect, soft skin and the pale pink complexion of a baby. I relished every insolent, triumphant moment of being eighteen, without fully appreciating how blessed I was. Women looked at me, women of the age Maman would have been, as if gazing at a memory, at ashes carried by the wind. Then some would smile, while others looked away – as you might when faced with a tragic scene, or a scar.

I was eighteen, without a care in the world, and this time the saleswoman at Nouvelles Galeries had persuaded me to try bolder lipsticks, in stronger colours. Drops of blood that men can't help wanting to lick, she whispered, goosebumps suddenly appearing on her bare arms. And I had the courage to try out Rouge Baiser, thinking Maman would have liked it too. She might even have suggested a thick slash of kohl across my eyelids, like those singers and actresses whose eyes bore straight into your heart. I loved the sense of being in bloom. I felt happy at this age that still smelt of milk and childhood, but was already tinged with the musky scent of lust and insolence. It felt as though I were poised somewhere between two versions of myself – but without any sense of being torn, just a perfect equilibrium. One that would never last, I knew, but that for the moment had a novel, fleeting charm, as short-lived as snow.

I savoured it just as later, before the pain and the terror, I would savour the permanency of things, the illusion that nothing was changing and that happiness was to be found in standing still for ever. I smiled while walking alone, without anyone ever taking me for an idiot. I smiled while climbing aboard the city tram, I smiled while looking at a dress in a shop window, I smiled when André came up to me in the street, in front of the Catho, when he asked me why I was smiling and I found myself unable to reply, other than with an even broader smile.

André wasn't the most handsome of boys, nor the worst-looking either. He had pleasantly sad eyes, a gentle way of seeing the world, like a prayer, a whisper. Like Gene Kelly's eyes in *The Young Girls of Rochefort* – that bit in the music shop when Françoise Dorléac comes in, moonstruck, a foregone conclusion. It seems to me the most decisive encounters are always the simplest, purely a matter of chance, a second's lapse in concentration, and suddenly there's someone else in our world, offering us warmth even though we hadn't realised we were cold.

André came into my life with his sad-looking eyes and I didn't go to lectures that day. We walked through Old Lille and I felt once more what Maman must have felt leaving Le Royal, leaving Anouk Aimée and Jean-Louis Trintignant. I, too, felt the urge to dance again; and André took my hand, made me do a *pas de deux* on Rue de la Monnaie. A few passers-by smiled – *aw, they're in love!* – and very nearly tossed us a coin or two. For the first time I felt my body discovering an emptiness. For the first time I sensed fear and fire in the pit of my stomach – and the carefree joy of having just turned eighteen now lay splintered and cracked.

That day André didn't try to kiss me or touch me. He made no promises at all. He didn't even suggest going for a coffee, or a hot chocolate, or a glass of wine. He simply unclasped his hand after our *pas de danse*, letting mine fly away, before it was finally his turn to smile, saying: if I don't see you again, it's because I'm dead. And I fell in love with these words immediately. He disappeared into the warm alleyways leaving me alone, both hungry for more and utterly fulfilled. And then the smell of milk, the smell of icing sugar when I was six, of mint cordials when I was eleven, of my first period at thirteen, my pain at having lived through it on my own, the scent of kir behind my ears at fifteen, on my neck, like perfume, a tiny drop of Maman, hidden away, and then later the smell of my first cigarettes and my first kisses – everything washed over me, flowing like a river along the pavement. All of a sudden I was pure, as pure as virgin snow; I had discovered fire and it seemed I'd never be cold again, and I began to laugh, the laughter of a newborn baby, an epiphany.

6

So, André.

Pure joy. A rock that would change the course of the stream.

He met me again a fortnight later, at Discorde where I'd just bought a few 7-inch singles. This time he suggested going for a drink. We went into one of the cafés on the Grand'Place in the middle of the afternoon and came out in the middle of the night, after many hours spent telling each other about our brief, mundane, glittering lives.

His family.

Farmers, in the Cambrésis. Twenty hectares of crops grown for fodder. A few animals. Nights with little sleep, hands worn away, blackened nails, like claws, weather-beaten skin, crackled old leather. Never any time off, never any May Days scented with lily of the valley; the earth, first and foremost, the demanding, fickle earth. And the sea, one time, only the one, for my seventh birthday, he explained, but not really the sea, more of a beach, at Étang des Argales in Rieulay – fine sand along the edge of an artificial lake on a former slag heap.

My parents hadn't wanted to disappoint me: they'd said there weren't any waves that day, some story about the moon, or planets, I can't remember – and I'd believed them, even though the water wasn't salty. Oh, that! said my father when I asked about the salt. It all depends on the currents, the tides and even the moon, André. It's very complicated, you see, it's all a bit messy. And later I learnt they'd wanted to write me a special story, one of a kind, to teach me that our imagination conjures up all manner of adventures, lifting our childhood to new heights of wonder.

They never complained, neither about the frost nor the rain that made everything rot. They furrowed and moulded the earth like sculptors, like lovers. They would talk to it, offer it thanks on days when the great harvests came in, console it when it was cracked and fissured by the cold; they liked the fact that time leaves its mark on the world. They waited for spring as if waiting to be forgiven. They were made to believe in pipe dreams, in the idea of being rewarded one day, in the promise of salvation and medals, for having given their lives to the earth.

They were lent money, in the name of a Common Agricultural Policy that would make rich men of them, proud men. Yes, they were lent large amounts, both they and many others, as if this were some kind of joke. And later, those greedy bankers turned up again, no laughing matter now, demanding their money. They wiped out entire families, razed family trees to the ground. Second homes devoured the land like a tumour. The French now wanted gardens and vegetable patches, barbecues, plastic swimming pools to fritter away their free time.

The army was trying to occupy more land on the Larzac plateau and the farmers became the villains, the spoilsports. People would talk about the American soldiers returning shattered and mutilated from Vietnam, but they failed to see our very own amputees, cut off from their rightful inheritance. Then something died in my parents' eyes and the day I turned sixteen my father, in a solemn voice, asked me to leave; he no longer had faith in a land that tore people to shreds instead of giving them nourishment.

I loved the words André used, his brutal yet gentle poetry. There was no anger within him, simply a sense of being resigned to the facts – and Gene Kelly's melancholy eyes. Society was changing, nothing more. No one knew anyone who could prevent that. Look, even your Luther King guy was assassinated, he said. Dreamers don't change the world, they just dream about it, that's all.

We ordered more drinks. Then it was my turn to speak.

My parents. The wobbly one and the one who'd flown away. The glazier and the dancer. A happy childhood

– barely two pages in a book. And then the ochre Taunus. The emptiness and the cold. Long John Silver trying to be a *maman*, but who spoke far too little for that; who didn't know how to braid a young girl's hair or choose her clothes, how to tell her she was attractive, or teach her to conquer the pain of growing up. You might have ten fathers, but you only ever have one mother, and when she's gone you've lost a limb for which there's no prosthesis whatsoever.

And finally my studies for an arts degree; my life as a student, both real and illusory at once. Those nights at the Pubstore spent raging against the injustice of the world, even though we were blind and deaf.

We were spoilt rotten – and rotten to the core.

That night, while I was trying to apologise to André for being so blind, he placed his finger on my lips. His skin felt rough, like very fine sandpaper; his touch reminded me of my father's hands. I told him about those broad hands, covered in cuts and gashes caused by glass and nails, splinters, tools, or by things he'd pick up without taking care, or those he used to break in the past. And then André smiled and I had the feeling I came from a place that wasn't so very different to his own.

I left the farm the day I turned sixteen. I learnt to shape wood, I became a carpenter and soon I'll be a skilled craftsman, a *compagnon*.

Compagnon. Like companion.

Partner.

The word took my breath away.

7

At nineteen, I was like all the other girls of my age.
We were in favour of abortion, moral freedom and sexual liberation. We wore bohemian dresses, bell-bottoms, midi skirts, floaty blouses, floral prints and psychedelic patterns, thigh-length boots and platform shoes: this was our uniform as warriors of Peace and Love.

We were Birkins and Joplins, Chers and Farrah Fawcetts. I had just gone into the second year of my arts degree.

The syllabus covered ethnographic and literary narratives, Chrétien de Troyes and medieval literature, English and Latin, with Proust still to come. I only saw André at weekends, and that too when I didn't go home where Papa – because of the intruders who'd taken to visiting the new houses while their owners were at work – had extended his services to include fitting security doors and various other locks that were reputedly burglar-proof. But Martine, those reputations don't mean much, he would mutter, grinning all the while. They're simply an excuse to have a good natter and pass on the bill.

Michel, for his part, had also left home, not to become a student but to move in with some of his pals. They were all living at a friend's place, doing up old motorbikes salvaged from the surrounding farms, a BSA Gold Star, or perhaps a Triumph TR6 Trophy. They imagined themselves as Johnny Strabler, Harry Bleeker and Chino in *The Wild One*, and became notorious as a bunch of hellraisers. They caught the eye of farm girls, whose hearts longed to burn with desire, and who dreamt of being swept away in the smoke and thunder of a bike. Girls who wanted to live fast and live dangerously, far from the land that was stifling them. Far from the beasts whose stench, inevitably, became part of them too – a terrible curse at dances and evening festivities at harvest time.

Papa seemed happy with Françoise. As I've said, there wasn't the same passion between them as there had been with Maman – that searing white heat – but rather a rare kind of friendship, a bond they shared at all times. I saw him laugh with her as I'd never seen him laugh, a laugh that echoed from the belly of the earth.

He had given up drinking.

Sometimes, he took Françoise to the coast, over by Bray-Dunes or Zuydcoote. He would say look how beautiful it is, look how tiny we are, and she would slip her arm under his, lean her head on his shoulder and sigh.

With the passage of time, Long John Silver had found peace with himself. He had let go of Maman. He no longer resented the cinema, or ochre-coloured cars. He had let his anger fly away, even if, from time to time, whenever his severed limb tormented him, he would still make a kir and place it squarely on the table.

There is no human sorrow that cannot become the source of love.

I turned twenty.

I will always remember the fifth of April that year: Brigitte Bardot had just told *France-Soir* she wouldn't be making any more films; that very evening, we organised an impromptu farewell party at the Pubstore. We'd all dressed in black leotards and tight green skirts with a long slit, like a guideline for the eye, a pathway for men's hands, feverish hands. And we danced to her bewitching, poisonous mambo, the one from *And God Created Woman*. In the middle of the night, a boy kissed my neck and lips, and I let him do it – I'd had one glass too many. We were all Bardots that evening, both gorgeous and deadly, and men's kisses were our compliments. Our bouquets.

I came home at daybreak, shattered, steeped in the pungent odour of desire.

André was waiting for me in my student room. He was twenty-six. He told me he'd be leaving to carry out his tour of France as an apprentice craftsman, an *aspirant*, before working on his masterpiece and, eventually, becoming a *compagnon* at last.

Being twenty suddenly took on a bitter taste.

8

At twenty-one, I was born for the second time.

My hair had grown again and I'd had it cut in the same bob as Romy Schneider, but more importantly I'd changed my name, swapping Martine for Betty.

I found it had a pleasingly English ring to it, with a touch of the folk singer too, and I was delighted by what it meant: 'Women called Betty are affectionate, romantic, emotional and lovable. Determined and optimistic, their positive outlook on life helps them overcome challenges. They are friendly and amiable, and one immediately feels relaxed in their company.'

Long John Silver looked at me, without saying anything at first, seemingly upset. Then he appeared to relax, reached out to stroke my cropped hair, my brow, my cheeks with his fingertips, as if trying to get to know them, and his face lit up as he made sense of who I was. You do look like a Betty, you're right. You're beautiful. Your Maman would be so proud of you. And me too. I'm proud of you, Betty. Betty, that's not just any old name, no it's not. It's . . . it's got style, hasn't it.

Papa had baptised me for a second time, welcoming me to this world all over again, and I was overwhelmed with emotion.

Martine left us that day. Someone else took her place – and it was the newcomer to whom Papa now spoke for the first time, allowing his words to blossom, crushing the embers that had burnt his mouth for years.

'I was twenty-four, Betty, hardly older than you are now, and I probably had the same dreams, but I'd been assigned to the third battalion of the ninth Marine Infantry Regiment, in charge of Psychological Action Services. It was the fifth unit, in the Bordj Menaïel zone, in Grande Kabylie – a place filled with mountains, coastal plains and proud men.'

Papa fell silent for a second; this was the longest sentence I had ever heard him say. He seemed to be pausing for breath, then he carried on, his voice more muted than before.

'We tortured everyone. Kids in front of their mothers.

Mothers in front of their men. Men in front of their sons. Electric shocks on their tongues, eyelids, breasts, genitals. I used to throw up watching them vomit. I would scream when they did. I was going mad. We were all going mad. Then the horror became addictive. A drug. We were drowning in muck. Filthy with rage. One morning, a child burst into flames, like a match. A little girl, eight years old. Shrieking. It stank like hell.

'I grabbed my gun from its holster. I turned it on me. Some of the guys were laughing. One of them rushed at me. I fell. The shot fired in the air. I was still alive and they transferred me to Palestro. I can still hear her, that little girl and her screams. When I came home, my leg had been ripped off, my eyes were shot with blood and your mother squirmed, ever so slightly. She was disgusted – and frightened. And it was all over.'

Then I took Papa in my arms, but the man I was comforting was that young lad, scarcely any older than myself.

9

André would write to me regularly.

He had examined the remarkable structure of the market hall in Questembert, from the sixteenth century. And studied the design of the storeroom and dormitory for lay brothers at the Château du Clos de Vougeot, including joists with half-lap joints and grooves, and central beams squared off with an adze (it was all Greek to me), before making a copy of the famous wooden bell from

Bourges Cathedral – also known as a semantron, a *tartavelle* or a *Balthazart*.

Then he'd settled down in the Jura for a few months to work on the various woods used in timber frames: Norway spruce – a soft, homogenous wood – along with elm, oak and chestnut, it's very similar to oak, he wrote, but without sapwood and redder in colour. He wouldn't discuss love but rather trees, angle braces, gussets and top plates. He wouldn't talk about seeing each other again but preferred to write about houses, canal locks and bridges. And I could tell, through his painstaking lists, that he was tracing a path to link us together, patiently reinforcing the obvious, constructing a love that was solid, carved to last a lifetime.

He liked the way time leaves its footprint on things, and I loved him for that too.

I was twenty-one, the precise age when Maman had said yes to Papa, on the twenty-eighth of June in Roubaix. In the heat and euphoria surrounding the arrival of the fourth stage of the Tour de France, from Rouen to Roubaix – 232 kilometres of sweating, shouting and cobbles, and roads lined with proud men and good-natured women. A Frenchman, Pierre Molinéris, had been first across the finishing line, in six hours, twenty-three minutes and nineteen seconds, and another Frenchman had taken the yellow jersey.

So then the man who still had two legs kissed the woman who was to say yes, the pretty woman next to him, for the first time – a kiss that sprang out of nowhere, amid the joy and cheers of the crowd, only to end in a life turned upside down. And I, now at the same smouldering age as Maman, I longed to have a partner – but some day, not immediately. I yearned to be part of a simple tale, the kind that never make great novels but are the stuff of real life. I dreamt of peace and having time. I dreamt of taking things gently. I wanted to carry on growing, to bloom alongside my partner as if in the warm shade of a tree. I wanted children, the scent of hot chocolate and, later, height charts pinned to bedroom doorposts and messy drawings. I wanted to grow old with a kind, patient man. And then one day be a grandmother – become one of those little old couples you sometimes come across in the park, on a bench, holding each other's hand, whose beauty has rubbed off on each other.

I had chosen André, I think. I loved his hands and the words he used. I liked the fact that he wasn't a student like the others I hung out with at the time: dreamers, rebels, smooth-talkers. I swung between my world, where life was merely described without really being lived, and the promise of a life that a man's hands would mould like clay.

Our story was taking shape like the title of a Jean Paulhan short story: *Progress in Love on the Slow Side*.

Maman had loved books and I loved them in turn in memory of her, along with art, photography, the cinema. She had even appeared in a couple of films. She'd been a butterfly, flirting with the light. She'd soared to dizzy heights and known the depths of despair, but she'd never dared fly too far. Far away from everything – from me, from Long John Silver. She'd always flown back, with her fevered cheeks, back to the coarse hands of a glazier who looked at life through window panes, just as she viewed it through cinema screens. She'd always returned to this raw, complex man, because he was one of those rare people with a feel for the flesh of things, who can sense the strength of the wind and paint you a magical world of your own.

My father had been that man before a little girl was set ablaze.

André had the same poetry running through his veins.

At twenty-one, I realised I was very like my mother – her twin, in my willingness to surrender.

I used to write long letters back to André. I'd tell him what I'd been reading, about crazy evenings at the Pub-store, or a Pink Floyd concert we'd been to in Paris in June and our epic journey back home. I felt he wouldn't have taken to that sort of music and those strange, unfamiliar sounds, given he was someone more used to caressing trees in the Jura, who'd learnt each of their names and could identify the winds from the way they whispered through the leaves. I didn't mention love to him either.

You don't mention fruit to someone who's thirsty.

During our time apart, I had a brief fling with an art teacher, a horrendous womaniser, the kind who'll assure you that you have the charm of a model, or the elegance of a portrait by Raphael. That you're a marvel, an oil painting from 1508 – that made me laugh! Who on earth do you think I am? Some young girl who's really, really old? No! I promise, you've got the sort of beauty that doesn't fade, you absolutely do. It's strange, Betty, very strange indeed. He awakened me to a cruder kind of sexuality, which I adored too, fanning the flames in parts of my body until they burned. He was the perfect lover.

A few weeks later, he happened to meet another

'model', a Botticelli this time, a Simonetta Vespucci, and we parted company as good friends. This was still a happy time in my life, a time when love was filled with joy.

I've kept a photo of myself, as a carefree young girl of twenty-one.

The art teacher hadn't been wrong.

But when you're twenty-one, you're blind.

10

At twenty-two, I found a job as a teacher in Bapaume, at Notre Dame Primary School, and began living my life the way others approach the end of theirs – a white blouse, a skirt down to my knees, an immaculate hairdo, the silhouette of an old maid, polite self-effacement and deathly boredom.

At twenty-three, André and I moved into a charming house whose frame and window casings needed renovation, a few kilometres from his parents' farm. They had left, exhausted and ruined, and gone to live in Valbonne, in the sunshine, in a little apartment – a shady balcony, no plants, no reminders of past suffering, nothing but sterile, sienna-coloured tiles.

André had created his masterpiece: a covered bridge on the Bouzanne, upstream from Saint-Gaultier. Crafted the old-fashioned way, assembled with wooden pegs, a bridge that was over twenty metres long, in oak and chestnut. And, from being an *aspirant*, he had become a *compagnon*.

He took me to see it one rainy day and I was terribly impressed. Then he got down on one knee, like they do in romances: a boy, a girl, a dark velvet box clutched in the boy's hand, a blissful smile on the girl's face.

At twenty-three, I said yes.

At twenty-three, like fifty-three million other French people, I also discovered the infinite capacity for evil that lurks within certain men. The heinous crime of Patrick Henry. The corpse of little Philippe Bertrand, rolled up in a carpet and left for several days in a bedroom at Les Charmilles – a hotel and restaurant on Rue Fortier in Troyes. The murderer declared on television that the criminal *deserved the death sentence for venting his rage on a child*.

It was enough to make you sick.

And then his defence lawyer, Robert Badinter.

And then the death sentence was put on trial.

At twenty-four, André and I were married.

The ceremony was simple and beautiful. André's parents had wanted the sweetness of Mozart or the joyful strains of Vivaldi and me, I'd wanted a song by Roberta

Flack. We finally settled on Saint-Preux, 'The Piano Beneath the Sea', and everyone thought that was perfect, both profound and light-hearted at once – like marriage itself, in fact. Maman's brother was there; it wasn't long before he was drunk and moody, and draped on his arm was a girl who resembled yet another popular singer – a twenty-something trophy blonde, a girl he paraded around shamelessly. Marion, Maman's closest friend, had come too. She was crying, saying you look so much like her, Betty. You're as pretty as a picture. I still miss her so much.

Françoise was wearing an elegant cream suit and a flowery hat adorned with fresh blooms that wilted rather quickly because of the heat, while Papa had hired a very classy grey morning coat. The new generation of prosthesis now allowed him to sit down without needing his hands to bend his leg, and he could finally wear *both* left and right shoes. Françoise was jubilant, forever ordering him Italian designs in fawn or black leather, as if taking revenge for all the years he'd had to hop around. She even asked André to make a cabinet for Long John Silver's twenty-seven pairs of shoes – leave room for fifty, you never know, she simpered. And my new husband happily fulfilled her request using some old Hungarian oak.

When Papa and I took to the floor for the first dance, to 'Only You' by The Platters, no one could have suspected that he was missing a leg, and I could tell from his eyes how proud he was to be a *complete* man at his daughter's wedding.

Michel hadn't been part of the celebrations and Françoise deeply regretted not being a family that day. So you have a child, she said, and he's nothing short of a disaster. He's a blot on the whole family, what a disgrace, me who'd always thought being a mother somehow immunised me against all this misery. Listening to her, I figured that Michel had come to cause suffering just as others come to bring peace; his instability, in a way, balanced out the natural order of the world.

He was serving a nineteen-month sentence in prison in Lens, for burglary. He'd been caught red-handed, ransacking houses whose occupants had gone off to work and gaining entry using copies of keys to the security doors Papa had fitted. Papa, incidentally, was placed under suspicion – and although his innocence was established very quickly, he ended up losing some business. Françoise, however, a diehard optimist despite the brutality and chaos around her, offered him encouragement: you love those glass panes of yours, why not have a go at picture framing? And that was how, a few months later, he opened a shop, Have it Framed, on Rue Desvachez, where he framed our wedding pictures and then, the year I turned twenty-five, photos of Sébastien, my son, who was born amid blood and screams.

God, how I missed Maman that day.

Had she been alive, I'd have dreamt she was by my side, holding my hand, reassuring and encouraging me, screaming with me, because she would have screamed with me, I know she would. She'd have panted for air in rhythm with me, she'd have felt hot and cold, she'd have called me *my baby* one last time – my baby, my little girl. And I would have been her baby one final time before I became a *maman* in turn. Before being afraid for ever after – afraid of a mosquito flying too close to him, of a curious dog coming too near, afraid of scarlet fever and cot death and germs at the nursery. Afraid he wouldn't walk when he turned one, or that his growth curve wouldn't be normal. Afraid of not knowing what to do, afraid he wouldn't love me, afraid of disappointing him – all those fears mothers have, which nestle in the same place as love.

At twenty-six, I'd lost the ten kilos notched up during my pregnancy and was even entitled to a bonus: two kilos less. I was lucky enough not to have a single stretch mark, thanks to the saleswoman at Nouvelles Galeries. I had regained my graceful figure, and I felt as light and fresh as May Day. I wore flounced miniskirts that were all the rage. I finally left my job as a primary school teacher in Bapaume to devote myself to our son, because André was often away, his expertise being much sought after on many construction sites – the restoration of the corn exchange in Martel, building the frame for a new church in Redon, or crafting the hull of a wooden clinker-built Folkboat in the south of England.

At twenty-six, I was the charming *maman* of a one-year-old boy, who was already walking.

A happy *maman*.

I was a lonely woman too.

II

Each reunion with my husband was filled with joy.

I loved the smell of sawdust in his hair, the smell of ferns and sap on his skin; I loved his impatient broad hands that would undress me – or rather, tear off my clothes. I loved his insatiable hunger for me, his sighs, his groans, the way he embraced me, smothered me, breathed me in like blotting paper sucking up ink – his gift for making me lose all sense of self-control. I loved the way he made love, fusing our bodies as one. He'd gaze at me, savouring the passage of time on my face. *You've been pining for me*, he would say, smiling.

He loved me and loved our child. He always brought him marvellous wooden toys that he used to carve, sculpt and paint during his breaks on building sites. He enjoyed being with his son. He would tell him about the forests and the wind. He taught him the words for parts of a tree: *crown, bark, sapwood, heart* – yes, Sébastien, the same word as for humans. He promised him days spent fishing together when he was older, tree houses, boats to conquer the seas, and our son would look up at him as if gazing at a king. We were truly blessed as a family – until the moment he left again.

This time he went to Saint-Denis-d'Anjou, to help with renovating the timber frame of its market hall. I discovered I was pregnant once more a few days later. But one night in May, my child, and all that it promised, slipped away between my thighs, sticky and streaked with blood. A night when all of France was in the streets, when more than 200,000 people, with roses in their hands, gathered on Place de la Bastille in Paris, singing and dancing – celebrating a Socialist victory, a reunion with the dreams of their youth and the chance to meet François Mitterrand, a man who wanted to *change life*.

I tried holding on to what was my little one, and I cried more tears than we were ever meant to have.

I was ill for several days but I didn't tell André about it. I won't ever tell him – men don't like to think you can die in the very place you've made love. And sometimes I find myself whispering to that child, to my baby who decided not to live with us.

At twenty-seven, the pain of this new loss put years on me again. And without a *maman*, you grow old the wrong way.

Michel had been released from prison. He was exceedingly thin and his eyes were choked with spite, Papa told me later. He'd gone round to his mother's and demanded all the cash she had, all her jewellery and silver, and threatened her with a flick knife. Papa tried to intervene. The robber gave his prosthesis a violent kick. Papa fell. His head struck the corner of a chair. The skin on his forehead tore open, like silk being ripped apart. The blood painted tears down his face. Françoise screamed and her son ran away.

Over time, and because of my frequent visits, the saleswoman at Nouvelles Galeries had become a good friend.

Odette was nine years older than me, but we were at that age when such differences don't count any more. She had a new man in her life, Fabrice. A good guy this time, she took pains to point out. He's in his fifties, and dependable. He's a photographer, a portrait photographer. He came up to me in the street. He thought I was *really hot*. He wanted me to pose for him, oh Jesus, what a session, what a session! In fact, he'd love to have you too (sniggering), have you pose for a photo, I mean – he's been working on some big secret project.

She was great fun, and a passionate advocate for all the new beauty products they would send her. I'm nothing but a guinea pig, she chuckled. One day, she tried out some false lashes that led to a few nasty styes, which she had to treat with a clove of fresh garlic. Another time, some fake tan turned her the colour of a boiled carrot. I look like a bloody twat, don't I? Like an Oompa-Loompa with added oomph! Odette was clear-headed: listen, you've only got what you've got, so I just undo a few buttons, the guys start ogling me down here, *et voilà!* Odette laughed and her laughter was sublime.

She loved life and loved her own life. Without a drop of jealousy or cynicism. She wanted her customers to be happy. Here, she said to me one evening as she pulled a new skincare cream from her bag, this is for you, for your baby-soft skin. It maintains your skin's natural balance – she was rattling this off – and slows down the emergence of wrinkles. It'll keep you looking young and beautiful – look, that's what it says. *Crème stabilisante.* By Guerlain, *ma chère.* You mustn't change a thing, Betty darling, you're perfect just as you are.

At twenty-eight, soon to be twenty-nine, my perfection had chiselled out a few wrinkles at the corners of my eyes. Invisible ones.

At three, my son, Sébastien, still revelled in that age when children love to say no – except when he was with his grandfather. They looked like a couple of kids with their very own language, without words or verbs needing conjugation, simply the same blood. It seemed as if Papa were finally able to quantify the joy of a new child, with its incredible promise of hope – this same man who hadn't wanted any more children after Algeria, not in a world that butchered its offspring the way trout savage their young. He liked to keep his grandson by his side for whole afternoons at a time and my son would remain there, within arm's reach. He didn't run around, or run away as he did with other grown-ups. He could sense this poor man was ailing and weak, and would bring things to him.

He brought the world much closer.

12

'Try not to smile.'

At thirty, I became a model for Fabrice's grand photographic project, ceremoniously entitled *On Time*.

For twenty years now, he'd been taking pictures of models every year, on a set date; one day, he explained, I don't yet know when, I'll turn this into a detailed study of how time affects the human face. Youth's fascinating, it's a magnet, and you feel so much pain when it's gone. The

GRÉGOIRE DELACOURT

model I started out with was twelve at the time, now he's thirty-two.

He showed me the twenty-one photos one after the other. The passage of time appeared to suit this man rather well. It flowed over him gently, like water.

Another face. A woman. Ten images. Over nine years, time had cracked her skin, criss-crossed the edges of her lips, like barbed wire, and hollowed out her cheeks, but it hadn't dimmed the sparkle in her eyes. It was striking.

A third. A young girl. Five photographs. On the second-to-last one, a scar had split her face from top to bottom, disfiguring her mouth. A motorbike accident, whispered Fabrice. On the fifth, total devastation.

'I hope time rekindles her happiness,' I murmured.

Even more faces, where a period of time, whether long or short, had reconfigured the map of their emotions.

Then, suddenly, a very old face. Only two images. Very little difference between the two, only the glow ebbing away, a darkening of the grey, the inevitability of it all. Ninety-six years old, said Fabrice. I was thinking of taking four more photos of him, going right up to when he's a hundred.

He'd persuaded me to take part in his project. You don't look your age, he'd said. It would be fun to try to capture the moment you do – and the words of that teacher, that expert on art and sex, came back to me: you've got the sort of beauty that doesn't fade, Betty, it's strange.

'Try not to smile.'

And I didn't smile.

I focused on his hand spinning around the lens, just as he'd asked me to. We carried out some tests with my hair

58

up, hair down, the collar of my blouse left open, then fastened; you need to keep this blouse in a really safe place – I'd like the same one every year. That made me smile.

'Try not to smile.'

And I didn't smile.

Later, he showed me the image he preferred, the one that would act as the point of reference for the shots still to come. And I couldn't help thinking about the portrait of Peggy Daniels, by Richard Avedon, in black and white, harsh and yet elegant, with its unexpected sense of presence. I thought I looked beautiful.

'Thank you.'

But photos don't tell the whole story.

13

At thirty, my face was still as soft and smooth as a child's, with gentle curves like a *madeleine* – just like Kim Basinger, Ornella Muti and Isabelle Huppert, who were the same age as me. But finer, sharper lines were now starting to emerge, tracing out the face I would have as an older woman. Going by the photos, I looked very much like Maman; she had had the same perfect, fine-grained skin, along with a few rare wrinkles at the corners of her eyes that seemed to spring from our laughter. She'd been the same age as me and couldn't have imagined – who could? – that she only had five more years left to dance.

She had left us her eternal beauty – every woman's dream.

At thirty, I was happy being with my husband, who now spent a fortnight with us every month. At the time, he was getting ready for a four-month trip to Italy, to hone his skills as a fully-fledged *compagnon*. He was going to work with the cabinetmaker Pierluigi Ghianda, dubbed 'the poet of wood' because of his passion for this astonishing living material, *which never dies, even after hundreds of years*. André beamed at the thought of meeting him. He gazed at his hands, the way he gazed at our son as he slept and sometimes at me. He would say: they haven't said everything yet, Betty, not yet. I know they've still got things to tell us, beautiful things. I don't yet know how, or what, but I know they have. André glowed with impatience. I liked the thought of his hands slowly revealing the harmony of the world, cultivating it, just as his parents' hands had once cultivated the earth and sculpted his soul.

And I, for my part, I loved those hands. I loved feeling them on me.

They set me on fire.

I missed them too.

Why not find yourself a lover? suggested Odette one evening when we were having dinner in a new brasserie. We were offered a drink on the house, a kir royal – *here's to you, Maman, to you, Betty* – to welcome us, a girl's night out, with a tad too much booze. Listen, there's no way I'd spend so many nights alone, not me. What a nightmare!

I need a man's weight, all of it, on my body and his rest-less fingers, crafty little devils, and his cool tongue, like a snake, twisting down through my skin, rooting around my hoo-ha. I almost spat out a mouthful of wine. You're nuts, Odette! Not in the slightest, *ma chère*. I call a spade a spade, simple as that, and men, well, they've got to be our greatest conquest. And what's theirs? Horses!

We were off to a great start. Men were staring at us, at her, at her mouth. Here, I'm no saint, I protested in a hushed voice, I've had a few affairs, you know, and there was that art teacher who . . . She cut me off. That was then, Betty, that was then. But I'm talking about right now, now that your carpenter guy's away fondling all that wood, sniffing around the leaves somewhere else. But how do you know? Ah, *ma chère*, do you really think a man who goes off for four months to a building site in Italy, where all the women are so hot, do you think he won't feel the urge? Go and ask the women who're married to sailors, or lorry drivers; all guys want is a tight little cul-de-sac and us girls, all we want is love.

A couple of tiramisus arrived. We ordered another carafe of wine. A medium? asked the waiter. Make it a large – and Odette carried on. You, with your pretty face, Betty, your peachy complexion, your cheeks as smooth as a baby's bottom, you'd charm anyone in a flash, even that bastard Fab. Oh, that son of a bitch! When he told me he thought you were *a dream to shoot*, I could've bloody chucked him out, I really could. Go on then, clear off! She put her glass down. But what can you do? I'm such a pushover, Betty. His answer to everything's the same. That angel face of his, those cheeky hands, those puppy-dog eyes after I've sucked him off, a sweet little compliment each time: you give the best blow jobs in the world, Odette. Well, seeing as I've not got your drop-dead looks, I've got to have something to drive 'em crazy too, haven't I? And we burst out laughing – but I'd gone as red as a beetroot, I have to say.

At seven, I'd seen my mother lose her sense of balance and my father plunged into grief. And I'd promised myself that if one day I had a partner, we'd both stand up to silence and anger. We'd stand up to *the wound and the knife, the slap and the cheek*, as Baudelaire puts it; so no, Odette, I won't find myself a lover. I'll never feel cold in bed, in that bed where André's not sleeping because he's off discovering the world, because he's digging for treasure inside himself with his bare hands. And no, I haven't found a lover, Odette, because love's just as much about anticipation and space to breathe, about patience and a sense of wonder.

Because it *is*.

14

On the precise anniversary of my first portrait, Fabrice shot the second one.

He'd set up the same backdrop of pearly-white paper, the same light, both harsh and elegant at once. I was wearing the same blouse. I took up the same pose as the year before: hair down, blouse slightly open, two buttons undone, hands placed on my hips, not smiling but with my lips one or two millimetres apart, looking just above the lens.

Click.

Fabrice compared the two images, scanning them closely for a long time with his loupe.

And I had the feeling something wasn't quite right.

15

We celebrated my husband's return at home; he was back from Italy, looking slim and tanned.

I'd made whatever Maman had had the time to teach me. *Goyère*, a cheese tart from Valenciennes. Roast beef – *rare, Martine, rare, otherwise it's tough as old boots* – flavoured with bay leaves and thyme, sprinkled with finely chopped garlic. A tart made with speculoos biscuits. Papa had taken care of the kir and André had sorted out the wine – he'd brought back a few delightful bottles of San Gimignano and Montepulciano. We raised a glass to everything we missed: a *maman*, a wife, a leg – and a son, added Françoise, sounding despondent for a moment. A little boy who should have grown as tall as a tree, straight up to the sky, swelling with pride and sap, not all twisted and tangled, like an octopus in the bowels of the earth. Papa hugged her close and whispered that from now on his grandson was her own and that I, his daughter, was now her own too. Long John Silver was sharing out the misery and the joy.

Over dinner, André regaled us with the beauty of Italy: its *piazzette* and churches, its nonchalant women and stylish men, and his eyes shone. After studying with Pierluigi Ghianda for four months, he had made a decision: he was going to create furniture, twisting wood as it had never been twisted before, stretching its limits even further. He dreamt of travelling to Scandinavia, to Sweden or Denmark, to study the bold designs of Jacobsen and Aalto, and others like Wegner and Møller, and we gazed at him, filled with wonder.

André was speaking a foreign language, the language of passion. And I adored him for that as well: this man, the farmers' son who wanted to beautify the world – and was beautified by his dream. The man whom I'd judged, the day we met, in the chaos of being eighteen, to be neither the most handsome of boys nor the worst-looking. This man, whose pleasantly sad eyes I'd loved straight away, eyes that had watched me as I entered his life. Thirteen years had passed so quickly.

Our son would soon turn six – still so small, already

so big; primary school, reading, writing and arithmetic. He understood the concepts of yesterday and tomorrow, according to the note from his teacher, even though he preferred the here and now. My son and his endless questions that had no answer: why don't animals smile? Why does it rain? Why don't I have a brother or sister? When I heard this my hands shook and it felt as if my fingers were turning to liquid – a slimy, scarlet substance.

Sébastien had fallen asleep on the sofa. He'd tried to hold his own with the grown-ups for quite a while, to keep up with their conversations. Will you take me to Italy, Papa, and to Candinovia? He had the pale complexion of an angel when he was sleeping peacefully and I knew that Maman was watching over him too.

We talked for a long time that night. We were happy.

But happiness, as everyone knows, is a fickle guest. It will sometimes leave the table without warning, for no reason at all.

16

At seven, Sébastien was 122 centimetres tall, weighed twenty-one kilos and had a head circumference of fifty-four centimetres.

Like Maman – and in some ways like Fabrice who, with his photos, was attempting to give the passage of time a physical form – I would note down my son's progress every year and reassure myself with the statistics. My husband used to tease me gently: I was a shrimp at his age,

Betty, and look at me now. Then I'd gaze at him, at this man who was so strong, and I knew that I'd always love him, both in his presence and his absence. That he was the one I had chosen, and that when I ran into other men in brasseries, or at the cinema, neither their smiles – so very charming, at times – nor their flirtatious words would ever tear me away from him.

At seven, I'd seen Maman cry because Papa's anger wasn't love any more. I'd seen Long John Silver lurching around on a single leg, with bloodshot eyes, his breath on fire. I'd seen him trying to grab hold of Maman to make her dance and I'd seen her curl up into herself, like an accordion.

At seven, I'd seen her flushed cheeks some evenings when she came home. I'd seen her kohl starting to run, liquid pain, tracing dark rings under her eyes. At seven, I'd seen how women suffer. I'd seen Maman slipping quietly out of Long John Silver's arms, as if fading into the background, before losing herself in other heady pleasures – including that euphoric sense of being alive.

At seven, Sébastien was now able to wait for something, calmly and patiently. He was starting to look forward to birthdays or things we had planned with a better sense of what time actually was. He could tell the difference between good and evil – evil's when you get caught doing something, he explained to me with a mischievous look. He was gaining confidence in himself and would spend more time lost in his imagination. André's absences brought us closer and we became accustomed to going out together, as Maman used to do with me – the cinema on Wednesdays, the Matisse Museum in Le Cateau-Cambrésis or the Natural History Museum in Lille on Saturdays. I showed him the most beautiful things men are capable of: the pain and suffering they had to overcome, their flashes of inspiration, the wonders that left them dazzled. Every once in a while, his questions would throw me: is this painting beautiful? What does beautiful mean? One day, in the park, he saw a woman older than me pushing a pram and he said it couldn't be much fun for the baby to have a *maman* that old. I asked him why: because when you're old, that means you won't last very long.

At almost thirty-two, because I wanted to last a long time for my son, I signed up for yoga lessons. The yoga teacher, Sādhu (Liliane-Berthe was her real name), maintained, as she observed me assume the curious and rather unappealing pose called Warrior II – *Virabhadrasana II* – that I had the body of a young woman of twenty-five.

All of the other girls agreed. Just one of them sniggered – jealous.

At almost thirty-two – while Sébastien was skipping happily into Year 3 and André, who was now travelling much less, had rented a barn a few kilometres from us, a place for him to shape wood and sculpt whatever his heart desired – I found a job, thanks to my arts degree, in the editorial department at La Redoute. We were not talking Anouilh or Prévert. This was a far cry from the dreams we had cherished during our feverish nights at the Pubstore, where we'd sit debating until daybreak, discussing the causes of Jim Morrison's death. Or that bastard Nixon and his attempts to hamper the struggle for equal civil rights. Or the tragedy of Vietnam, while drinking, smoking and making love without love. No, these were merely a few words placed here and there, below flattering images designed to showcase the fashions for spring/summer 1985: cotton skirts, fresh new colours and bold patterns, swimsuits, low-cut backs and daring necklines, the latest materials, bikinis.

To begin with, I tried educating my readers with a few key facts – so *bikini*, for example, came from the name of the American atoll where a nuclear test had taken place, which gave Louis Réard, its inventor, the idea of launching it with the slogan: 'The bikini, the first anatomic bomb'. Afterwards, they asked me to be more discreet with my knowledge and keep it to myself.

That year, we were celebrating Odette turning forty and her new job: the exclusive representative for a fledgling brand of cosmetics. AuDelique, *ma chère*, as in oh-so-chic, for the entire Nord-Pas-de-Calais region – twelve thousand five hundred square kilometres. Just imagine! We were celebrating André's first chair, in Brazilian rosewood, whose arms, with their incredible twists and turns, resembled lava. It was truly magnificent – so much so that Odette wanted to sit on another chair so she could admire it – and I was proud of my husband, proud of what his hands had revealed. We were celebrating Sébastien's forthcoming eighth birthday. We were celebrating the success of Brigitte from yoga, who had finally mastered the tricky pose known as the Wide-Legged Forward Bend, *Prasarita Padottanasana*. We were celebrating Long John Silver and Françoise, bound together as never before. And, above all, we were celebrating the sheer joy of simply being alive – in André's barn, in the meadow, on the surrounding roads lit by paper lanterns, like a fireman's ball.

We were dancing outside, pleasantly drunk, and Sébastien, who'd been encouraged to have a tiny sip of beer by his *papa*, began to see fairies and even Mickey Mouse, but he wasn't completely sure . . . maybe it was Clarabelle. Long John Silver was dancing too; he managed not to trip up Françoise. And Maman's absence weighed heavily on me that night. We were dancing to Peter and Sloane, Cookie Dingler, The Star Sisters, and André held me tight against his firm body. The smell of wood and ferns hung over us, the scent of happiness. He whispered that he loved me as much as the day we'd first met. Your hair was so short, Betty. You had cherry lips and you'd just turned eighteen. He told me he'd always loved the comforting, *slow* pace of our relationship and my patience; and I shed a few tears, but I think it was because of the rum in the sangria.

Which stung my eyes.

17

At thirty-two, I discovered the pleasures of Valbonne – the Place des Arcades, the former abbey church and the Gruss Circus during the August holiday weekend.

My in-laws had aged bit by bit, the way you shuffle towards death – it seemed that the absence of earth beneath their feet, the absence of rain and wind and hail that sometimes ruined a harvest season, a year, a whole existence, had left them shrivelled and dry. There wasn't a single plant on their balcony, no flowers in the apartment, not even in a painting, not even on doilies. They had torn themselves away from their previous life, the way you remove a tumour by burning everything around it, and were now waiting for the end, but with no sense of despair.

We stayed with them for a few days.

André insisted on taking them to the Fondation Maeght in Saint-Paul-de-Vence, where he stood transfixed before the Giacomettis, Braques, Calders and Mirós, and felt a yearning for iron and bronze. At midday, we had lunch at La Colombe d'Or – Picasso, Léger and Soutine were on the walls, poached sea bass and rack of roast lamb on our plates. You shouldn't spoil us so, muttered Renée, and André placed his hand on his mother's, a tiny little hand, dry and grey, a pebble, which disappeared immediately under the broad, powerful hand belonging to her son. It's all thanks to you, and Papa, that my fingers have the Midas touch, so let me thank you in return. At that moment their eyes shone and there was nothing more to be said between them.

We spent an afternoon at the beach, a place I didn't like at all. Sébastien couldn't go swimming because of the jellyfish. He made castles out of pebbles with his father, since there wasn't any sand – let's build a tower up to the sky, Papa! Later, he went off to sit beside Renée and, more importantly, her cool box, for chilled lemonade and sweet-tasting fruit.

André and I slipped away and went for a romantic stroll along the water's edge. I noticed women whose skin had been worn and faded by the sun, with the colour of caramel, the smooth texture of a cigar, as silken and glossy as chocolate. And others, the skin on their faces stretched as tight as a drum. Their bodies lost in the illusion that youth was the only possible kind of beauty, that their appeal would slowly evaporate with time. André gave me a mischievous smile; he made me promise never to be like them and in return he promised he'd always love me just as I was, as I would be when I grew old, and we went back to join his parents.

Our son was deep in conversation with his grandfather, listening to stories about the farm, the seasons, the animals. He asked him whether their cows had had names. Because it must be sad to eat something that has a name. The old man ruffled his hair: you're just like your father, aren't you? But no, no one ate Églantine, Violette and Iris. They died of old age, they were over twenty-two, in a big field full of grass and poppies, buttercups and butterflies. And twenty-two, that's a good age for a cow, you know! I thought about how lucky we were to be there, together, alive, even though we were sitting on burning pebbles, even facing a sea infested with jellyfish, because nothing lasts for ever and that very certainty is a precious key in itself.

At thirty-two, I was exactly half the age of screen legend Simone Signoret who'd just left us – she'd flown away, her pancreas completely destroyed.

In the autumn, Odette got engaged to Fabrice – at least I'll have some lovely wedding photos, she said, laughing. André created an outstanding chair in which he also made use of iron, so overwhelmed had he been by what Giacometti had done with it for his sculpture *Dog*.

Sébastien went into Year 4 – a proper little model for La Redoute – and at the company they applauded my work on the upcoming catalogue, Spring/Summer 1986. I was congratulated for no longer peppering my product captions with scholarly personal reflections and, most importantly, I was given a rise – I would be able to pay for André's trip to Scandinavia.

At yoga, I had now mastered to perfection the poses known as the Triangle, *Trikonasana*, and the Locust, *Salabhasana*. Sādhu was astounded that her art, in my case, had led to a second flush of youth. She later informed me, in a hushed tone, like an air hostess, that the price of her lessons was about to increase, because unemployment within the active population had just crossed the nine per cent mark. But I don't get it, Sādhu? Patience, young grasshopper, I've got a proposal for you: if you'll agree to pose for my new flyer, I'll let you stay at the old rate. But why? Seriously, take a look at yourself – no one would think you're as old as you are.

Upon which I assumed the pose called *Savasana*. Otherwise known as the Corpse.

18

The twenty-third photo showed him at thirty-four, still as handsome, year after year – a serene beauty, not a shadow in sight.

The twelfth portrait of the woman now revealed a face that was tattered and torn; this time, her mouth was surrounded by a dense mesh of wrinkles, like brambles, but she still had the same sparkling eyes – a victory for her, I thought.

The seventh photograph of the young girl who'd been in an accident revealed an unexpected smoothness around her scar, as if water had flattened out the rough surface of sand. The happiness you'd hoped for, whispered Fabrice.

This year there were three new faces, three new images.

First, a little girl of two, with blonde curls and plump, shiny cheeks, like two apricots. He'd had to wait for her to go to sleep before shooting a portrait he could replicate every year – and every year to come, on the same date, Fabrice would again have to wait for her to fall asleep. I found the whole thing quite bizarre and quite insane.

Then, some guy he'd met in a bar who'd just got out of prison. A face that, at thirty, was already a scene of devastation, covered in tattoos, like the hieroglyphics of misery, a mini atlas of his fall. I really hope he'll play along every year, the photographer confided. He wanted a thousand francs for this photo, can you believe it!

As for the third face, it belonged to a young woman. She looked a bit like Odette would have done at twenty-five, with mottled, milky-white cheeks – and I suddenly feared for my friend.

And then me; my fourth portrait, at thirty-three – and still the same pearly-white backdrop, the same light that had made Peggy Daniels so hypnotic under Avedon's gaze, the same white blouse, which I only wore on this occasion, hair down, hands on my hips. Try not to smile, Betty. No smiling, look just above the lens. Over here, look at my hand, I'm wiggling my finger. Fabrice compared my pose to the one in the three previous photos. He came over to ruffle my hair a few times – it had grown – and finally managed to get what he wanted. He showed me the latest portrait; of course, it looked like the three others and – had you glanced at them briefly – you might have thought they were all exactly the same. That's the point, he explained enthusiastically, it's like those flip books with a whole series of pictures – they're almost identical but you get the impression of movement as soon as you flick through.

However, the fact that my face had apparently remained unchanged made me slightly uneasy. I thought about that last photograph of Maman, the Polaroid her friend Marion had given me, nearly twenty years earlier. I thought about how happy she had looked, her ginger fringe, her Cardin dress. Maman who was so beautiful, immortally beautiful, whom no amount of time, nor any malice in this world, nor weariness, could ever tarnish again.

The dead don't grow old, she'd said when the two of us had run off to Paris for the weekend, because at home Long John Silver's fury had sent chairs and tables flying and crockery whirling in all directions. And at the Louvre, she was overcome with emotion as she showed me a painting by Raphael, *La Belle Jardinière*, or *The Beautiful Gardener*, also known as *The Madonna and Child with the Infant Saint John the Baptist*. Look at this woman, Martine, look at the purity of her face. That's what she's left us. She'll never be old. It's incredibly moving. There's something there that challenges death itself, don't you think?

I was eleven at the time. I hadn't grasped that she was telling me about the heartache women endure. The primordial fear of time wiping you away, changing and dissolving things all the while, until it's erased what had once been your charm and elegance and desire – in fact life itself, everything, leaving nothing but ashes, nothing but the fear of the loneliness still to come.

Dear God, I'd have given anything for Maman to still be there, even covered in wrinkles, or scratches, or scars. But still there, with us.

I didn't like my fourth portrait.

It looked like the portrait of a corpse. A face that wouldn't change any more.

19

Impatienta doloris.

At thirty-four, I learnt this was the cause of melancholic suicide – linked to what used to be called neurasthenia.

I had blossomed into a woman of thirty-four during a tragic spring; our beloved Dalida, the nation's songbird, had left a note: 'My life is unbearable.' People sobbed in the streets, sweet words soared through the air, while others, the scathing ones, landed with a thud.

Françoise and Papa made the trip to Paris, because Dalida had been a *grande dame* for Françoise and if you don't say thank you to those who've brought you joy, then you're nothing, nothing but a miserable wretch. It was cold that day, as cold as a heart left to wither and die. They couldn't get into the Church of La Madeleine; at Montmartre Cemetery they'd had to wait for four hours, on three legs, before they could throw a white rose from some distance, which was trampled on immediately. But when they returned home, exhausted, Françoise wasn't angry that everything had been meant purely for celebrities, with nothing for the common people, not a word, not even a smile. Nothing but metal barriers, like you'd have for pigs; that's just how it is, she said, that's all, but it doesn't stop us from caring.

I had no one but Odette with me to celebrate my birthday, because André had been away for a couple of months now, in the Bordelais. He was working on a huge construction site – a frame in oak heartwood of impressive dimensions: sixty metres long, ten metres high, in the shape of an inverted double hull, a wine storehouse to accommodate the finest *grands crus*. I don't know how you do it, *ma chère*, but you haven't changed a bit, said Odette the moment she saw me. You'd pass for your little sister if you had one, or else it's because you're waiting for your man – it must relax the skin. I wasn't bold enough to respond by saying she hadn't changed either, because with each passing year her eyes and cheeks were sinking more and more, and her complexion was turning grey.

She sensed my discomfort.

I think the thousands of kilometres I'm clocking up in

the car are killing me, this fucking sales agent lark, you've no idea. All those nights in stinking hotels, those station cafés where everything's gone off, guys clinging on to you – pathetic little guys, like those puppies at the dog home whining for you to stroke them. And sometimes I end up stroking them, Betty. Sometimes I say yes, I say yes so I won't be alone any more, to feel alive and young, and I hate myself each time because Fab really *does* love me. He's no cheat, he calls me his princess, he thanks me every time he's had a blow job, one of my 'princess specials'. Oh, it makes me want to cry, I feel like scraping myself with sandpaper, I want rid of the shame.

I took her hand.

Look, even though my skin's starting to sag – see here, on my neck, under my arms, and don't even *start* on my breasts, that bloody law of gravity – he still thinks I'm beautiful. A beautiful bitch, oh yes. A beautiful bitch.

She and Fabrice still hadn't got married – he was the one who liked a long engagement, who liked each of them being able to say of the other, *he's my fiancé, she's my fiancée*. He liked their relationship to remain a promise, a hope, and in any case, that word, *fiancée*, it gives women who're not yet engaged something to dream about, she added, sounding defeated, especially when you're my age.

At forty-three, she was still working for AuDelique. What a crap name, Betty, you just can't imagine: I've got women asking, what, like Angélique? and men saying, what, like fucking piss, *eau de leak*? I feel like resigning, chucking it all in, all this shit. I want to grow old with Fab, to become a little granny one day, because when you're old, the beautiful thing is being old, pure and simple.

And I couldn't help thinking about the young girl who looked like her, the model in Fabrice's photos.

André came home the following month, looking happy, like a sailor who's enjoyed a safe crossing and returned with a purse full of gold, and a few other treasures, for his son and his wife. We had an evening, a whole week of celebrations. Sébastien, perched on his father's knees, asked him for more, tell me more, and I gazed at the two men in my life with infinite tenderness and love, praying that nothing would ever cast a shadow over our bliss.

Later, in bed, I offered myself up to my husband as I'd never dared before, without holding back, without a trace of modesty. I surrendered myself, all of me, to his restless fingers and ravenous mouth, and gave in to his urges and desires, both daring and new.

Michel and his band of thugs were arrested by the *gendarmerie* again, shortly after assaulting a couple in their eighties whom they'd duped into believing they were police officers to enter their home. They'd resurrected some old-fashioned tricks, tying their victims up like *saucisson* and torturing them with red-hot foot warmers; they'd sliced off three fingers with secateurs to get hold of three rings, ripped off two earlobes for two earrings and soiled the entire house.

Françoise did not react. She didn't scream or shout. She didn't smash anything around her. She simply took Papa's hand. She said take me somewhere, somewhere there's only beautiful things. Please. And Long John Silver wrapped her in his arms, held her tight against his heart and took her to Tuscany, to a place that breathes the artistic genius of man and God. A place where the fields ripple beneath the wind, like the sea, where the cypress avenues trace out paths that lead to the sky, where the cool air of churches will dry your tears.

They stayed there for a long time, even looking at houses for rent and for sale, far from the roar of bikes and gangs of hooligans, in villages where you could leave the door open and the bread on the table. Françoise soothed her maternal anguish with the beauty of the world, and when her son was handed a heavy sentence, she wanted nothing more to do with him. I'm not the first *maman* to lose a son, she whispered gently.

And I saw Papa cry.

20

'Stunning!' exclaimed Fabrice when I entered his little studio.

I'd cut my hair the day before so it would be just as it was in the first three photographs.

I put my blouse on again, leaving the top two buttons open. I positioned myself in front of the pearly-white backdrop, in the light that was harsh yet elegant. I placed my hands on my hips. I didn't smile. My lips were slightly

open, one or two millimetres apart. I focused on Fabrice's
finger, bobbing around above the lens.

The sound of the shutter.

A blinding flash.

The sixth image.

At thirty-five, my life was turned upside down.

Thirty to Thirty

21

The six portraits were lying on the table.

Six faces in black and white. The same. Mine. One image every year, six sessions over five years. Time passing by so quickly. Sébastien growing up. Long John Silver losing the last of his hair.

It's extraordinary, said Fabrice eventually, look, just look! And I knew what I'd known instinctively for some time already, even if I couldn't believe my own eyes.

I knew the chaos this foretold.

I knew the joy and bewilderment still to come.

I knew my good fortune and the hell of damnation.

It was captivating and terrifying at once.

'Look,' repeated Fabrice, 'it's the same face.'

'I know.'

'I mean, the same, Betty, exactly the same.'

He grabbed six sheets of clear acetate on which he'd printed my six photos, placed them on top of each other and held them up to the light.

'Look, apart from the tilt of your head, which isn't quite the same in each shot, and the angle of the arms that's slightly different, and your hair too, you've had the same face for five years, Betty. It's mind-blowing. The same. Time's got no hold on you. Doesn't leave any mark. Your skin's the same. Your skin's texture is the same. Five years and not one wrinkle, nothing's faded away. It's sublime.'

Odette gave a discreet cough behind us. She was holding a bottle of pear liqueur. This is sublime too, she said. It's only eight years old but it's already an old lady, and she laughed. A hollow laugh.

At the age when Maman's youth had engraved itself for ever on one last Polaroid, when her beauty had been carried away by an ochre Ford Taunus, frozen mid-flight just as an artist's brush had frozen *La Belle Jardinière*, something within me froze as well.

From the age of thirty, I had stopped growing old.

22

My husband and our son are asleep.

I get up and lock myself in the bathroom. Sitting on the rim of the bathtub, I examine my face in the large mirror. My hands tremble as I touch the skin on my gently curved forehead. I skim my cheeks with my finger, searching for my cheekbones; I squeeze my lips. I trace the silky circumference of my mouth, my chin, then the edges of my jaws. I run my hand down my neck, over my shoulders, my throat, over my firm, round breasts – I remember fondly how Jean-Marc Delahaye, in his impatience, had savoured their delights in his room, watched by the road racer Giacomo Agostini pinned to the ceiling. We were seventeen and would be young for ever.

I stroke my flat stomach, its taut, satin-smooth skin, my finely sculpted hips, my long, pale thighs (thank you, Maman), and my eyes fill with tears, which I can't hold back. I recall the comments made by Sādhu, the yoga students and Odette: you never change, *ma chère*. And what my lover *par excellence* had said when I was twenty-one: you've got the sort of beauty that doesn't fade, Betty. It's strange, very strange indeed. I'd assumed these to be no more than sweet little words, honey poured into a young girl's ears.

I recall a promise too, one that André had made on the beach at Nice surrounded by faces that had lost this war, after I'd just asked him if he'd always love me as I was, as I would be when I grew old, and he'd sworn he always would. Had he already sensed I wasn't changing, this man who could detect beauty yet to emerge simply from the trunk of a maple tree? This man who would stroke my face with his coarse hands, the way you might stroke a patch of burnt earth – and who knew how to rekindle its magic, how to heal the scars left behind by days and nights spent without him. This man who made the brittle anxiety of waiting melt away, and loved all that was revealed by the passing of time.

I look at my face in our bathroom mirror and I smile.

So here I am.

Here is my face, across which time flows like clear

water. My face, like *La Belle Jardinière*, in the Louvre, which Maman had found so moving, always twenty years old, every single day for more than 500 years; that face, eternally young and gentle, benevolent and smooth.

Here I am, a monster and a miracle.

Here I am, every woman's dream.

And I start to laugh. Thinking about the joy that is mine from now on, the joy of finding myself so pristine, so pure each morning, of basking for ever in the euphoria of youth, which is the promise that everything is possible. I shall dream without fear of a cruel awakening. I shall enjoy life without the fear of passing away, without the terror of ending up alone.

Growing old is painful and brutal. It means letting things wither away and being helpless to do anything about it, like the silkiness of our skin and its milky-white texture. It means seeing it become spotted and blotchy, starting to loosen and sag.

Growing old means seeing our place on Earth shrink bit by bit and watching our shadows begin to shrivel. It means that, in the end, we'll vanish completely.

So here I am.

Here I am, still young at the age when our youth slips away.

Here I am, a rare curiosity.

We all, each of us, examine ourselves every day. And every day we see ourselves as young. And even when the light's not very flattering, we *know* we're young.

I read somewhere that you don't see yourself grow old. You put your first wrinkles down to muscular hyper-activity – you call them expression lines, incidentally, which is a lot less nightmarish. And you drop your guard. You don't notice the grid pattern etched by time, now starting to show on your face, creeping up on you – horizontal, vertical and lateral wrinkles, level with your eye sockets, whose colour is, however, rather flattering. Crow's feet – *rays of sunlight*, any old rubbish.

Then you buy yourself a magnifying mirror and you tremble a little, because *that* certainly wasn't there last week. You notice the skin and muscle around your eyes are now distended. That your upper eyelids – which you loved to paint in shades of grey and bronze, and dust with gold on party nights – feel heavy. They're now decreasing the sharpness of your eyes, diminishing their appeal (we'll make an exception for Charlotte Rampling), and you put on your distance glasses, moving a little closer to the terrifying mirror. Only to discover, at the level of the lower eyelids, that the fatty deposits that once sat in line with your eye sockets have slipped and, on this horrifying morning, form bags under your eyes. Bags filled with tears, tears you'll weep over time dead and gone, the battle now lost, the eternity that is no more.

It's hard to pick yourself up after a tragedy. It drives a blade through your heart.

Then you stuff your face with Prozac. You treat yourself with other antidepressants too, or even go under the knife. You look at photographs from when you were twenty. You try to look like you used to be again. Then you end up throwing in the towel, just as others might throw up their arms in despair.

The anguish I will never know.

It's getting brighter outside and – as if someone's opening

a shutter – the bathroom is gradually flooded with light.

I can hear my son going down to the kitchen; he's always the first to get up. I hear the sound of the fridge door, the milk jug knocking the table, chinking against the rim of a ceramic bowl, the chair legs scraping along the tiled floor.

I splash some cold water on my face.

I don't have any rings under my eyes, no shadows at all.

Youth offers the additional benefit of masking your sleepless nights.

André knocks at the bathroom door. I'm coming, darling; I'll be down in a second.

But first, and with a pleasure that can't be described, I shall throw away everything that's cluttering up the sides of the sink: creams labelled as anti-ageing, anti-wrinkle, lifting, relifting, re-plumping, tightening, along with eye and lip contour serum. I'm going to throw everything away – all except my moisturising cream and sunscreen. Those are your basics, says Odette, your basics: *without them, you're dead*.

Then I shall join the boys in the kitchen.

So here I am.

23

Hagop Haytayan – our family doctor ever since we'd been a family – burst out laughing.

But there's no such thing, Betty, not growing old! Everything grows old. Men, women, trees, plants, dogs, thank God. Even your hoover, your TV, songs – often theories do as well. André's growing old too. But not me. But not you. He became serious again. But not you. Have you talked to him? No. Good. Let's start with a blood test, shall we, and we'll take it from there, based on the results. Then he smiled again, a smile that made his eyes sparkle. I think you're imagining things, Betty.

At thirty (thirty-five), my levels of uric acid, albumin, gamma-glutamyl transferase, cholesterol, creatinine, blood sugar, haemoglobin, thyroid-stimulating hormone and triglycerides, and my erythrocyte sedimentation rate, were all completely normal. X-rays of my bones showed the same thing: my bone mass had remained stable since the age of twenty. It would begin to decrease after I turned forty, they explained.

An MRI chopped my body into slices and found nothing wrong whatsoever, apart from the fact that it was obviously that of a woman of thirty-five in very good health. A dermatologist examined my skin from every angle while sucking on some candied angelica – bad breath? – and reckoned it was thirty at a push. When I told her I was a good five years older, she began to examine me again and finally blurted out: that's odd – you've got an epidermis that's clearly younger than you are. She had a long discussion with Dr Haytayan; they exchanged some files and complicated words with each other, and concluded that, while it was impossible to say with certainty that I wasn't getting old, just as I'd claimed (with my photos to back it up), it was nevertheless acknowledged that my skin had all the qualities – the absence of wrinkles, elasticity, firmness, lustre, et cetera – to be found in a young woman of barely thirty. Even if internally – in terms of my organs, muscles, bones, et cetera – I patently had the body of a woman of thirty-five.

I wasn't growing old on the outside. I was growing old on the inside.

My husband hadn't noticed anything and nor, for that matter, had our son. A few women, however, at the yoga class, noted with envy my glowing complexion, my youthful appearance, my baby-soft skin, all of which Sādhu was only too quick to credit to her teaching. May I remind you, ladies, that the ultimate aim of all our efforts is liberation, *moksha*, from the cycle of rebirth, *samsara*, that springs from each person's karma, and Betty's rebirth is going very well. Oh yes, very well indeed.

Odette assumed the beauty products she'd been giving me were responsible for this miracle, that a reaction between the chemicals in her creams and those in my skin had in fact produced some kind of alchemy, something no one had ever seen. They ought to use you for research, she laughed, like the Wild Child, in that Truffaut film, or the Elephant Man. Well, thanks a million, Odette. Oh, sorry, I'm so sorry, that's not what I meant, what I meant was . . . Yes, I know, Odette.

She still hadn't resigned from her job as a sales agent for AuDelique products – it's killing me, I'm telling you, it's killing me – because Fabrice was going through a horribly slack period. Ever since cameras had become widely accessible, cheap and disposable, everyone aspired to be a photographer, churning out pictures of everything around them, from monuments and their friends' faces to little town squares, pigeons and the odd teardrop or two. And very soon endless images of the dish of the day, pasta with bolognese sauce, plates of brown shrimp, on and on until you felt sick, would feature in the albums of our lives, telling our stories, charting each family's journey.

What else would we pass on to our children, other

than our shallow view of the world? Other than thou-sands of useless photos that gave everyone the impression they were talented and signalled the slow demise of the professional photographer? Fabrice's income had dried up and Odette was now working twice as hard. Her eyes and cheeks were sinking even further, she had taken on a permanently ashen complexion and her age – all forty-five years of it – was rude enough to make her look at least seven or eight years older.

People get dumped for less, Betty.

On her birthday she was in floods of tears. Fabrice and André tried to comfort her with the clever words men are known to use, sometimes in all sincerity, to make a woman believe she looks a lot younger than her age. That she's absolutely stunning, that in fact the passage of time simply adds to her beauty, that she's more attractive now than she ever was at thirty, or even twenty. You're a bunch of liars! You're all bastards! Yes, Odette, yes you are. And no, come on, pull yourself together. Just look at Juliette Gréco, said Fabrice. She was fifty before she was drop-dead gorgeous and really sexy, not when she was younger. Oh, do you think so? But didn't she have her nose redone?

24

At thirty (thirty-six), I floated in the heady glow of my secret. I was giddy with youth, I basked in the present and it seemed I'd never speak in the past tense again.

At thirty (thirty-seven), I made the most of the final hours of my son's childhood, the last cuddles, those last shared moments before the first rugged signs of manhood: the voice breaking, the first wisps of body hair, the need for independence.

That summer we went to stay with Françoise and Papa, who had rented a house for a year in Tuscany, in Pitigliano, a village built on a cliff of volcanic rock. From their terrace the view over the gorges of the Lente was both dizzying and soothing. It made them forget about the missing leg and the son locked up in Poissy Central Prison. They were happy: beauty is an antidepressant.

When we parted company after a few magical days together, Papa looked at me curiously, then said goodbye, Paule.

Paule. Maman's name.

I felt my legs give way.

Perhaps we turn into the people we miss. Perhaps we fill the void, through fear of leaving it empty. Perhaps we crystallise the essence of what they were so as to keep them with us for ever.

'Goodbye, Paule.'

At thirty (thirty-eight), I saw André overcome with joy at the press launch of his first collection of tables and chairs. He dedicated it to his parents for having taught him about the earth and the stones, the raging waters and the mud, the magnificent violence of nature. The high-end label Cassina had made the furniture and was now distributing it everywhere; the collection soon became a sensation, not only in France, but also in Germany, Sweden and the United States.

My husband was fulfilling his dreams. Time loved him.

I was only too aware of how women were starting to look at him and he was equally conscious of their gaze too. Of how they would sometimes bite their lips as they watched him, as if clutching a sheet, or stifling a cry. I found it all rather obscene and quite sickening, but he would always put my mind at ease and that made me want to weep every time.

Not only was I loved, but I was also his favourite.

One morning when I woke up – and after his coarse, precise fingers had made me come – he told me again that I was beautiful and added, for the first time, *you're still the same, Betty*.

This was an alarming sentence.

Had he noticed I hadn't changed? Did he sense what I was keeping to myself, what on the one hand seemed like a dream and on the other a total monstrosity? If he knew, would he think I was sick? Abnormal? Would he be horrified by the idea that I might suddenly grow old, for no reason at all? Until now, neither Dr Haytayan nor anyone else could explain what was happening to me – their lack of knowledge offered me a kind of reassurance. And when I thought about André, all of this terrified me: would he still love me?

It's you, you do that to me, I ended up saying. You're the one who keeps me young. It's all for you, André. He smiled and climbed out of bed. You're an amazing woman, Betty.

Sébastien was going to be thirteen. He was in secondary school, in Year 9, where the new curriculum stated that *commitments outside of school ought to enable young people to build a foundation for their personal lives and professional careers, and become responsible citizens*. So we signed him up to a football club, where he proved to be a rather gifted goalkeeper. On weekends I would teach him the names of artists, writers and a few film-makers, and from his father he learnt about fishing, silence, patience and different species of tree. He slipped into adolescence with no drama and no crisis, just as I had once slipped into it myself – and I know that the gentleness, kindness and even the friendship of his father had a lot to do with it.

Françoise and Papa returned from Italy. They went back to their house, to new neighbours, vicious dogs, kids running wild, broken windows and a few new round-abouts. Their days as retirees would spiral downhill from the moment their neighbours went off to work, descending into a brooding idleness, a blanket of silence, a sombre mood. And one afternoon, while I was visiting them, Papa took my face in his hands and tried to place his lips on mine.

25

At thirty (thirty-eight), Fabrice shot my ninth portrait. The same light, the same pearly backdrop, the same blouse and still no smiling, Betty; like Peggy Daniels.

The image confirmed that after eight years, I didn't, as they say, look a day older. Not a wrinkle.

It's me who's getting them instead of you, muttered Odette, disillusioned.

26

At thirty (thirty-nine), I had, like everyone else, listened endlessly to Jordi Savall's viol, because of Alain Corneau's film *All The Mornings of the World*, and then, like everyone else, I'd gone back to other music: Cyndi Lauper, Queen, Emmylou Harris.

One lunchtime, in a restaurant where my husband and I were eating, a couple were watching us closely. Then the woman whispered something in her partner's ear. I sensed this had upset André and he stared at me in turn for a second, with a look I'd never seen on his face, full of melancholy.

I didn't pay much attention and now I know this was a mistake.

Papa underwent a series of tests in hospital. His memory was clogged up, like those drawers so chock-full of things you can't even open them any more. His recollections were muddled and confused. He fixed his gaze on me several times, while we were having lunch or sitting in the garden, and began to cry. Tears ran down his face, but he didn't wipe them away.

Sometimes he asked where his leg had gone. If he'd been born like that. If it would eventually grow back.

And then it was Françoise who'd start to cry.

Odette caved in. She was going to be fifty in less than two years. Younger women, prettier and more resilient (little tarts, indeed), had their eye on her job; and anyway, I'm not a complete moron, I can see it all. Fabrice drooling over those little sluts – it's not models for his book he's looking for, he's looking for what I've lost, Betty, and once you've lost it, that scares men away. And so, in the hazy light of dawn, without breathing a word to anyone, least of all to her fiancé, she went off to a private clinic to have her face and neck lifted.

She came back forty-eight hours later, with a few pale bruises on her skin. She came back full of hope and love, but her fiancé refused to take her in his arms, or even speak. She promised him, with a strange, sad smile, that having her skin tightened wouldn't change a thing, not even her mastery of the special gift she had. But Fabrice remained withdrawn, like a child shocked by being burnt for the first time. His lips quivered, the words refused to come out and then there was silence, a dreadful, murderous silence of the worst possible kind.

They would have to get to know each other again, try to invent new words and gestures, some new way of naming all this.

The devastation that claimed to be love.

27

At thirty (forty), I was moved to tears by a piano washed up on the sands of New Zealand, moved to tears by the pain of Jane Campion who, only a month after her Palme d'Or, lost her eleven-day-old son. 'People asked me how my baby was; my breasts leaked milk.' And I caught myself hoping he was with my own child who'd decided not to live here, with us.

At thirty (forty), I organised a huge party for my fortieth.

All the girls from yoga were there, with their husbands, a few copywriters from La Redoute too, where I'd been appointed creative director, *eh oui, ma chère*. Some of the *mamans* and *papas* of my pupils from Bapaume, parents with whom we used to enjoy a good laugh. And some former students from the Catho, whom we'd tracked down thanks to the alumni association. We had the girls from our years at the Pubstore, from that crazy Bardot night spent in black leotards and green skirts. We had the pretty boys from back then, the touchy-feely guys, all hands, the smooth-talkers, who'd neither redefined the world nor gone off to join the anti-apartheid campaigners in America or South Africa. Who'd allowed their rebellions to slip by the wayside and their bodies to grow heavy and bloated. And who'd become insurance agents, company bosses, lawyers or consultants, because you need to make a living, to support your family, maintain a certain status, pay off the mortgage and put some money aside for a week's holiday with Club Med. Or to buy a Porsche one day, just to remind everyone you're still young at heart.

One of them came up to me. I recognised him at once and my heart started racing – the little snake; he congratulated me on my *daintiness* and I fell for the word immediately. It was about as old-fashioned as you could get. Then he asked me where he could find Betty, whom he assumed must be my big sister given our resemblance. It's me. He sniggered. No, I don't think so. Betty's at least ten years older than you. I smiled. I knew her really well, you know; I even think she was secretly in love with me. His words echoed inside me, piercing, stabbing at my chest. You knew, I muttered, you knew but you still left her all alone, pining for you? He frowned, then whispered: there's something quite flattering about being desired. And something quite obnoxious about exploiting it, I interrupted.

I don't get it, he carried on. Has Betty told you about me? If she's as pretty as she used to be, I'll try to make up for it. A woman will always forgive a stupid mistake, Christian, but never the pain of missing an opportunity in life, so no, you're not having a second chance with me again, not ever. I left my broken heart back at the Pubstore, on those fake leather seats, a very long time ago.

His crystal-clear eyes narrowed, staring at me. Betty, oh my God, Betty, it *is* you. You haven't changed a bit. It's incredible. He ran his fingers through my hair and I shrank back. I remember you had it cut very short, like Jean Seberg in *Saint Joan*, and you had skirts that flew up in the air. I chose them for you. And your eyes, those looks that would flutter towards me, I've been such an idiot. Selfish, more like.

My God, how is it you've not grown old while we've all aged so much? I should have married you. Stop that. Then I wouldn't have had to leave you for someone younger. That's enough, Christian, you're not being funny any more. I felt so hurt when you ignored me, but that's all in the past now. I'm happy, I love someone and they love me back. And we even have a son, a terrific kid. What about you? I'm guessing you never became the great director you dreamt you'd be, a Godard, or a Truffaut?

So you remember that too, Betty? Yes, you're right,

I didn't become a director, or else you'd have heard all about it. Just the boss of a printing firm. We do supermarket flyers, annual reports, wedding menus. Married? Divorced, twice. Are you happy? Do you really want to know? No. Could I see you again, maybe a coffee one day? No.

He hung his head and half-opened his mouth but not a word came out. Then he was swept away, engulfed by a tide of guests dancing, drinking, laughing, reuniting with friends, mingling with each other – and my heart stopped pounding.

Later, the Catho alumni, all slightly the worse for wear, sang Neil Young's 'Ohio', the song that had been our anthem. Some of the girls from yoga came to join them and my eyes welled up, filling with tears, tears that carried along with them those carefree years, those happy years when we never took stock of the extraordinary good fortune we had to be alive. At that moment André came and pressed his lips against my cheek, soaking up my tears. His arms wrapped themselves around me, pinning me against him, and I knew, once more, that he was the love of my life.

I went over to join the yoga girls who were writhing to the music like serpents and driving the boys crazy. I later had Misraki's mambo played several times, the one that had turned Bardot into a global superstar and scandalised the National Legion of (In)Decency. And we felt just as we had that first day. Feverish, bewitched, we were the very embodiment of desire. We were the Devil himself – and the Devil wore a mask of utter madness.

Odette glided from arm to arm, occasionally stroking

men's cheeks – tell me I'm gorgeous, big boy. A mixture of drunkenness and high spirits had flung the cage wide open. The words came tumbling out and Fabrice didn't go looking for his fiancée. He didn't ask her to hold back – he knew she was simply trying to prove she was still good at snaring men, at driving them insane. If you can't move you might as well be dead, he said to me, horrified.

A few of the Catho girls were determined to find out what make of skincare products I used, the address of my surgeon, where I went for yoga lessons. They wanted a list of foods I ate, what yoghurts, what fruit, what brands of water. I assured them I didn't do anything in particular and they called me an ungrateful so-and-so. Have you forgotten that we cried together for Vietnam? We even took you to see Pink Floyd in Paris! It's disgusting, what you're doing, Betty, absolutely disgusting. Keeping it all to yourself, a secret like that – the secret to staying young. Imagine that! Girls, honestly, I swear to you that . . . and we collapsed in fits of laughter.

It was a glorious night. It drew to a close, sadly, as dawn broke. A few people headed home, but most of the others, including my husband, Odette and myself, staggered joyfully, still dancing, to the nearest bistro. We sat on the terrace and bolted down a hearty breakfast, laughing and joking one last time, promising each other we'd meet again. Clinging on, for one final hour, to everything that was sliding from our grasp.

Christian got to his feet, his knees like jelly, limbs shaking. He raised his cup high in the air and, with a foul, cottony taste in his mouth, announced: I propose a toast to Betty and with your permission, André, to her beauty and her youth. She's the only one here who's stayed young, while we've all turned into old fa . . .

He never finished his sentence.

He crumpled to the floor, sublime, pathetic, drunk.

28

At thirty (forty-one), my body's stock of ovarian follicles ran out and this, combined with a gradual reduction in the secretion of my progesterone and oestrogens, affected my mood. I went through periods of feeling sad and anxious. I had more frequent migraines, my breasts hurt, I experienced hot flushes and – to my husband's delight – my libido shot up.

The perimenopause, diagnosed Hagop Haytayan.

Already? I asked, but how is that possible? Do you think I'm growing older more quickly on the inside, to compensate? He gave me a sympathetic look. You're one of the ten per cent of women to whom this happens prematurely, Betty, so no, this isn't some compensatory phenomenon. And in any case, you're lucky. You're also one of the less than one per cent of women who don't gain weight during this period. Having said that, I admit that talking about the perimenopause to a woman of thirty does seem bizarre.

One morning, when I woke up, André was sitting on the bed. He was looking at me.

I didn't have the courage to ask him why.

Sébastien turned sixteen. He was beginning to drift away from us, bit by bit, while trying not to hurt our feelings. Growing up is brutal – you need time to grieve and it's painful. You want to be free and independent but still enjoy the security you had as a child. You start banging your head against the walls of this world, sizing up the space you'll occupy some day.

One evening, when his father had gone to Sweden again for a few weeks, he asked me if he was good-looking, if he was attractive, if others would fancy him; and anyway, how *do* you meet someone, Maman, how do you know? The next day, I took him out to revamp his wardrobe, inviting him to choose whatever he wanted. He emerged from the fitting room sporting the mod look – a button-down shirt, a two-piece suit, a jacket with three buttons, drainpipe trousers – and fired a question at me: if you were young, Maman, oops, I mean if you were my age, would you go out with me? Yes, Sébastien, yes, I'd find you really handsome.

I was pleased he felt he still needed me.

Odette had had collagen injections in her lips. You see, Betty, my mouth just didn't go with my face any more. Nice fleshy lips are so much sexier, and – according to the doctor – they help soften your nasolabial lines.

I was sixteen when our paths had crossed for the first time, at Nouvelles Galeries, where she was a saleswoman. At the time she was twenty-five and although she was no beauty queen, she had a sparkle, a *joie de vivre* that made you want to be with her.

My heart ached for her.

Surgery is an addiction, a hope that never dies: after your face it's your lips, after the lips, the eyelids, after the eyelids, the breasts, after the breasts, the stomach, after the stomach, the knees. And time passes and you start all over again to pass the time. You see yourself as getting younger and younger, more and more beautiful, more and more perfect, while in fact others see you as a miserable wretch.

Fabrice no longer viewed her through the eyes of a man but those of a photographer, and it was through those eyes that he came to cherish her physical disfigurement. Something that purported to be a mark of love, almost an act of submission, a sense of belonging – like the body scarring that connects the Guiziga people of Cameroon to each other. Odette had become an image that fascinated him, a *subject*. And as for me, I loved my friend. I loved her fear of no longer being beautiful enough, no longer young enough in the eyes of her fiancé; I liked to think she loved herself at last.

André's father died that year, from a ruptured aneurysm. A little grenade in his head. We buried him in Nord, in soil rich in clay, the kind he used to prize because it swelled up, then shrank again. Like a man's heart, he said, it's alive.

There, I shall turn into earth once more.

I shall become the Earth.

At thirty (forty-two), what had been my good fortune was about to bring me nothing but misery.

29

For twelve years, I had had the face and appearance of a young woman of thirty.

Today, I was forty-two.

For twelve years, I had stayed the same and no one in my neighbourhood had been surprised in the least. You can tell a man's changing because he's had hair implants, or he's suddenly bought himself a sports convertible, or he's flaunting a woman as young as his daughters. You can tell a woman's changing because she puts on weight, dyes her hair or starts wearing lower heels. But if you stay the same, precisely the same, people are blind as can be, perhaps because they relish the thought that they themselves don't change either – *the mirror effect*.

For twelve years, I had felt a thrill every morning. For twelve years I had seen my immaculate face reflected in my husband's eyes, or in the bathroom mirror. I had delighted in compliments; I had smiled all alone as I walked, as I had at eighteen. I had lived the dream of being youthful and fresh-faced – and remaining so, without a single beauty product or the surgeon's knife, without any explanation.

I was like a promise that would be kept for ever.

For Odette, this was clearly linked to Maman. You realised you weren't growing any older at the very age she died. You stopped growing old so you'd stay younger than her. And maybe even – who knows? – to make your father suffer, or quite the reverse, so as not to leave him on his own. Oh! It's all so confusing!

For Fabrice, however, the key was more likely to be found in poetry and magic, in accepting those miracles that happen without us knowing why – like the beauty of flowers, or the power of redemption.

But for André, this had gradually become something abnormal and unsettling, since even if official records stated we were only six years apart in age, a gap of almost twenty years was now plainly visible between us.

One morning, he finally asked the question.

'What's going on, Betty?'

I couldn't bring myself to say anything. My heart was racing. One more word and I'd have started to cry.

'What's going on, Betty?'

And then I sobbed uncontrollably.

'Things can be terrifying when they don't have a name. Is it a rare disease? Some sort of regeneration? You haven't sold your soul, have you?'

'I'm scared, André. I'm so scared sometimes.'

He wiped away my tears, the rough flesh on his fingers scratching my cheeks, and I noticed something new in his eyes.

Shortly afterwards, he had me examined in Paris, by some top specialists who'd been recommended to him.

I was analysed from head to toe. I had several biopsies in several parts of my body. I was scanned. I was sliced by a laser. I had tubes inserted here, there and everywhere. I was made to do the Rorschach, Beck and Coopersmith tests. They scratched their heads. They locked themselves away. They huddled together.

But they found nothing more than a body in a rude state of health, that of a woman of forty-two who had the beguiling appearance of a young woman of thirty.

On the way back, André remained quiet for a long time. I knew him too well not to know that his heart was thumping, that he was hovering on the edge of that sickening sense of fear that can sometimes ruin your life. We had been together for twenty-four years, we'd fallen in love, I had remained a faithful wife, even when he was away. I had given him all the time he'd ever needed, my patience and my faith, so that his hands could reach the treasure buried within him. I'd always supported him and had never lost heart when he left for months at a time, making do with letters filled with unfamiliar words, *jatoba*, *kauri*, *olon*, *ramin*, *cerejeira* (I found out later they were the names of different types of wood – there was no end to the things he was learning). I had turned his son into a kind-hearted, polished young man, a blessing to us all; I loved them each and every day.

When he finally opened his mouth, my world fell apart.

'I'm leaving.'

30

Naked, words can sound incredibly violent.
    'I'm leaving.'
Two words with not an ounce of fat. Two dry little bones. A blade, more than a sentence.

You don't have a nervous breakdown in a car racing along at more than 130 kilometres an hour.

I remained calm.

I turned to look at him – his eyes were glued to the

motorway. Then I saw the years I hadn't wanted to see on his face. The silvery hair on his temples, the first rusty spots on his hands, the bags under his eyes, the wrinkles that remained in place when he wasn't smiling, the cheeks beginning to sink a little, giving him a gentle appearance. I saw the years that separated us, that had flown by so quickly, barely enough time to compose the myth of a man, or the jubilant song of a woman. I saw agony, I saw our paths diverging. I didn't cry, but anger drilled its way through my stomach.

What you're doing is disgusting, André. You're nothing but a coward! Loving someone means loving everything about them. I loved you every second of every day, even when you weren't there, even when you were silent, or went too far. Then I looked down and stopped glaring at him. My love's unconditional. It's always there. Yours is so fickle. You're leaving because you don't like what's happening to me. That's just pathetic. It's ludicrous. In fact, there's not even a word for it.

He swallowed this quietly, without flying into a temper. Then he spoke. Why all these years of lying, Betty? What made you think I wouldn't notice, I wouldn't be worried, I wouldn't be concerned about you? I turned away, staring out at the scenery, and I suddenly felt so empty. So ugly. He carried on. I'll be straight with you. I feel cheated. Because you lied to me. But even more because you're not changing at all. Yes, I agree, loving someone means loving everything about them – loving them as the years roll by, even when their bodies start to change. I'm a man of the soil and for me our seasons are vital – you can't live in spring for ever. But you never said a thing. I respected your silence, I bottled up my questions and I waited. I waited for you, Betty.

I dreamt of growing old with you, living through the century by your side. I dreamt of seeing you grow old slowly, gracefully. Watching you curse as you pulled out your first grey hairs, making funny faces to firm up your skin, seeing autumn's colours appear on your hands and our finest years blossom in your face, painting a picture of our lives and all the joys we'd shared. I thought I saw a tear welling up in his eye.

It's horrendous, what's happening to us. Horrendous. I've always loved you, ever since your first smile, on Rue de la Monnaie. But you've also got to face up to things. I might not feel happy living with a woman who's twenty years younger, or twenty-five, someone who'll be thirty years younger one day. I don't want snide remarks, or dirty looks, or people being jealous. I just want my wife's age to tell our story, to prove we've spent a quarter of a century together – has it really been so long? My God!

I had dreams, like you, Betty, and I've not forgotten anything you said. About becoming one of those little old couples you sometimes come across in the park, on a bench, holding each other's hand, whose beauty has rubbed off on each other. But you can't be a little old couple when one of you is forty years younger than the other. You wanted to become a grandmother, making hot chocolate, but you can't be a grandmother at thirty, Betty. You can't be a grandmother if your son ends up being older than you, if one day your husband's the same age as your father and then as old as your grandfather.

I was about to say something, to try to redeem myself

in André's eyes. I know you'll always be you, Betty, you'll always have your soul that I love, the same heart, but I think, deep down, that I'm terrified of seeing you staying the same. It's as if you were the shore and I'm drifting away. You're a constant reminder I'm going to die.

Then I began to sob. My hands started to shake. I curled up on the seat. I wanted to disappear, to open the door all of a sudden, to toss out this body that wouldn't grow old, to let it be crushed by the cars and lorries. I wasn't even mad at my husband. I understood his pain, his disappointment. I asked him to forgive me for having said nothing about my affliction, for not having had faith in him. I told him again how happy I'd felt simply being beautiful for him, and young for him. That I loved him, that he was the love of my life, that I would never, ever leave him.

He stopped five minutes later in a lay-by, well away from a handful of parked cars, in the shade of some trees – I recognised the blackthorns, he'd taught me about them – and we cried as we made love.

And that was all.

31

We miss our *mamans*.

Mine had had arms that would gather me up, that knew how I felt, that took care of me. I would have loved one last chance to cry into those arms, to snuggle up, to hear the words *I'm here* once again, to hear once more I'll always love you, Martine, whatever you do.

I stayed with Françoise and Papa for a few days. I arrived in tears and it felt like I'd suddenly grown very old – my body ached all over, like a woman with arthritis. *Old: adj. a person who feels useless, experiencing a sense of loss and neglect, fatigue and insomnia.* I needed to drum up some courage but, ironically, it was my pain – the very same pain you can't keep choked up inside you, or you run the risk of drowning – that gave me the strength to tell them André and I were separating. Papa raised an eyebrow. But you've already left, Paule. You went off with my leg and my love and Martine.

Françoise rushed over to me and opened her arms, arms that hadn't held a child for more than eight years, not since her own son had been sent to prison in Poissy, where he'd never agreed to see her although she'd visited numerous times. She wrapped them around me as if folding her wings around some poor soul who's trembling all over. She whispered some long-forgotten words in my ear: my baby, my sweetheart, I'm here, Betty. Go on, cry, tears will wash it all away – tears are nothing but the seeds of hope. And I slipped into her warm embrace.

Later, she told me about her divorce, about the bastard who'd left her – for some younger woman, oh yes, that was *him* – and about wanting to die, then meeting Papa, at Le Chat Noir. There's a story waiting for each of us, Betty, there always is. Something you can't predict. Something that sends you spinning. He had come in for rubber boots and when he'd found a style that suited his left foot, he'd asked if she could hold on to the right one and send it to the Red Cross for the poor lads who'd been blown to bits by anti-personnel mines, in Vietnam, Cambodia and Laos. It was his sensitivity, his tender feelings for men who were suffering, that's what melted my heart, she confessed.

I realised Françoise had been living with Papa for more than twenty-five years. I was sixteen when they'd got married. She'd been through every phase – the glazing, the security doors and then the framing shop that had seen its finest hour when one of the Mulliez sons, of the Auchan group, had had 270 of his wedding photos framed there, with a feature in *La Voix du Nord* and all the other papers too.

Françoise had been a buttress for Long John Silver all those years, she'd always caught him before he fell, but now, Betty, now I don't know what to do any more. He's crumbling inside himself, he's sinking. I've nothing to hold on to. He keeps asking where his leg's gone, why I'm crying, and some nights, when I cuddle up against him, when I try to stroke him, to comfort him, he'll start to howl. That evening I was the one who took Françoise in my arms and whispered some long-forgotten words to her.

One night, I was woken by hands touching my breasts, feeling for my belly. My arms flailed, shearing through empty space, and finally struck someone's body. The body fell onto the coffee table, which broke under its weight. I put the light on at once.

Papa.

Françoise came running.

I love you, Paule, said Papa. Come back. Please. I won't break any more things. I won't shout any more.

At thirty (forty-two), I was the spitting image of Maman.

In the eyes of Long John Silver, I was her. I was the serpent and temptation. I was the very thing that was devouring him.

Sébastien decided to go and live with his father. For the same distressing reasons – the other day, they asked me if you were my big sister. Soon, they'll be asking if we're going out, Maman. One day they'll ask if you're my wife. I didn't stop him from leaving. But I still love you, Maman. I know. Growing up is brutal – I've said it before. You need time to grieve and it's painful.

You grieve for the weakest.

The two men in my life left me because my everlasting youth was a monstrosity. Because it's not normal to remain thirty for thirty years; because it's crucial that whatever we have loved degrades one day. That the image we had grows dim, little by little, fading away, to remind us how fleeting it was and how lucky we were even to have caught it, like a butterfly in the palm of our hand. Things need to perish so we can be certain we ever possessed them at all.

I was the one who left in the end.

32

At thirty (forty-four), I felt as though I'd aged overnight.

I found I could no longer decipher the instructions on medicine or the use-by date on a yoghurt.

For several months now, reading a book, or a magazine, had become a challenge, as had reading a menu in a restaurant. And I was loath to buy one of those pairs of ready-made glasses you find at the chemist's, somewhere between the condoms, the cough sweets and the pregnancy tests. Those glasses that immediately, and inevitably, make you look old and burdened down by life. All of a sudden people don't look at you the way they once did. One little accessory betrays you, exposing your frailties, the decay that's still to come. It robs you of your elegance and lightness of touch. Clutched in your hands, it slows down your movements.

You'd like to make it disappear from view and your fingers close around the shameful object like pliers, ready to crush it, to rip it apart like a piece of paper, to fling it under the table. It's a reminder of something within you that you don't like any more. Age holds you captive while freedom recedes into the distance. You begin to feel afraid. You're watching out for those first spots on your skin, the blue outline of your veins, or a finger that no longer extends as fully as it should.

But I didn't have any choice.

One morning, while I was shopping in my local convenience store, I needed my glasses to read the ingredients on some tabbouleh – I'm not a great fan of anchovies – and a shop assistant came up to me, terribly pleasant, asking if she could help. I tried to distract her: these glasses are funny, aren't they! Someone's left them on a shelf. I just wondered what you could see through them. She peered at me and I was about to make my escape, feeling a bit sheepish, but then she smiled. I did think they couldn't possibly be yours. So I handed her the glasses and dropped the tabbouleh with anchovies into my basket.

Later, I got into the habit of using my phone to take

photos of instructions or lists of ingredients that I'd enlarge so I could read the fine print.

You can lie to other people; lying to yourself is more difficult.

33

'You need a recent photo, it says it here.'
    'This *is* a recent one.'
'How recent?'
'From this morning.'
'So you're telling me this – in inverted commas – "recent" photo corresponds to the person by the name of Rousseau, Martine, Françoise, Claude, ex-wife of André Delattre, born on 17 January 1953, in postal code 59400,

Cambrai, Nord? Who's aged, if I'm not mistaken, forty-four, since it's 1997, even though the face in this – still in inverted commas – "recent" photo appears to be barely thirty?'

'That's correct.'

It was only then that, from the other side of the glass, the middle-aged woman who was dealing with my application glanced up from the form, for the renewal of my national identity card (CERFA number 12101*02, to be completed in BLOCK CAPITALS and without crossings-out), and finally looked at me. She hesitated for a second. A flicker of alarm. Then she looked at the two photos lying in front of her once more.

'That's you?'

'That's me.'

'But you're not forty-four.'

'Yes, I am. Ninety-seven minus fifty-three.'

'Sir!'

'I . . .'

'Sir!'

It took less than a minute for the boss to appear, two minutes for the woman to explain the situation to him, and five seconds for their eyes to flick between my face and the photos again several times. It was the boss who spoke next, wearing a cruel smile – the kind a boss would have.

'Look, I've had women through here who've tried lying about their age. Oh, a few months here and there, fudging things by a year or two. They'll say a three's really an eight, or fiddle with a one so it looks like a seven, wanting to make themselves younger. I can understand that – it's simply pride, vanity, even despair. But trying to make out you're older than you are, Madame, um, Rousseau, Madame Rousseau, especially by more than ten years, I have to confess there's something I don't get here. It doesn't quite add up, to be honest. You're not your own daughter, are you? I mean, this lady's daughter?'

It was all very complicated.

Thank God, the boss had a boss, a woman as it turned out, who grabbed the form, the supporting documents and the notorious photos, and asked me to accompany her to her office, where she invited me to take a seat and offered me something to drink – water, that's free, coffee from the machine, fifty centimes. I'm fine, thanks. Then she asked me to run through my story again.

In the afternoon a stream of people filed past one by one: André, Sébastien, Odette and Fabrice, who had to swear on their honour that I truly was who I claimed to be. Hagop Haytayan was contacted by telephone. He solemnly confirmed the affliction I was suffering from – a medical enigma, Madame Deputy Commissioner, that would sooner or later deprive me of the joys of old age, of those affectionate nicknames such as 'granny', 'gran' or even 'grandma'. Thank you, Doctor, that's all very clear.

Late that afternoon, the 'recent' photo was endorsed and my application to renew my identity card was approved. The deputy police commissioner came out onto the pavement with me, apologised for the matter having been blown out of all proportion and invited me to have a drink in the bar opposite, The Crooks, which I accepted, somewhat amused. I ordered a kir – *cheers, Maman* – and she asked for a neat bourbon.

Before the waiter could bring us our drinks, she focused her eyes on mine – her heart, I imagine, was pounding like a drum – and said:

'Martine . . .'

'Betty, please.'

'Of course, Betty. As you wish. But give me the name of your anti-ageing cream.'

34

At thirty (forty-five), I'd been living for more than two years in a large studio, on Rue Basse.

I had lost the desire to cook, I'd discovered ready meals for one at Picard and whenever my son came for lunch I had his favourite sushi delivered.

André and I had remained friends. He was spending more and more time in Sweden – where he would choose his larches, aspens and spruces – and, when he returned, he never failed to call or invite me to dinner. I would sit there bewitched every time by his sad eyes. You're Gene Kelly, I'm Françoise Dorléac; I still loved him, I had always loved him.

I used to draft my copy for La Redoute while watching TV shows: *Dawson's Creek*, for my sloppy side, *Dr. Quinn, Medicine Woman*, even though she really got on my nerves, *ER* – sigh, Doug Ross – and *Twin Peaks*. I hadn't thought about getting a cat or a dog, because when they turned four they might well have resented me being younger than they were. I whiled away my evenings at yoga and became the queen of the Reverse Warrior pose, *Viparita Virabhadrasana*, and the challenging pose known as the Bow, *Dhanurasana*. Take a look at Betty, exclaimed a jubilant Sādhu. You should all be inspired by her.

Odette and Fabrice often dropped by – we're your tranquilisers, *ma chère*. They would bring *gâteaux*, *saucisson* and wine. She was still working for AuDelique: so listen, I stood up to those little sluts – they were just running around like headless chickens – and hey presto, they got me a new car, an Opel Corsa! It's so cute – they even let me choose the colour. She'd gone for a cream that went with her newly dyed platinum hair.

Fabrice took pictures of her constantly: when she was eating a salad, taking a sip of wine, tucking back a wisp of blonde hair, throwing herself into my arms, or adjusting her bra in which her new breasts were desperate for air – *after the breasts, the stomach, after the stomach, the knees*. Perhaps I'll turn them into a book one day, he said, on the theme of the creation of the self, and I made no comment of any kind.

On Saturdays, at lunchtime, I'd go and eat with Françoise and Papa. Afterwards, he'd disappear for a nap in a horrid electric recliner, covered in brown imitation leather. Françoise would do the dishes and then pick up her knitting again. She was making pullovers, scarves and woolly hats for the inmates at Poissy, where Michel was a prisoner. But I've no idea what happens to them, she sighed, whether the guards pass them on or keep them for themselves. And as for me, I'd flick through the magazines that were lying around, with my reading glasses perched on my nose, and I noted every week, to my horror, that now I really was living the life of an old maid.

That was the last straw.

I began going out again, sometimes with one or two copywriters from La Redoute, but the fact I was their boss prevented us from being completely open with each other – so I mostly went out with Odette. We would go to the Pubstore in the evenings, a mojito for her, a kir for me. The place had kept its originality. 'We've changed everything so everything stays the same' proclaimed their new slogan, but you no longer ran into those fervent style-conscious idealists from my years at the Catho: Jean-Paul, Céline, Christian, Laetitia, Liza, all of us. The kids who had once redefined the geography of the world, discussing literature or the Nouvelle Vague, getting fired up about Malcolm X – no, none of that.

Instead, you now came across crafty old foxes, who'd encircle their prey before homing in, ties undone, wedding rings stashed in their trouser pockets. They skulked around, offered us drinks, came and sat with us; our visible age difference unsettled them. Are you friends from work?

Cousins? Lesbians? The ravenous ones always swooped down on Odette. She egged them on, laughing obligingly at their lame jokes – and I'm being polite; sometimes, after a third or fourth mojito, she would let them fondle her, her knees, her thighs, then she'd forcibly remove the intrusive hand with a roar of laughter. Seriously, are you crazy? I'm *engaged*! And everyone would be tickled pink and wanted to be engaged to her, despite her being fifty-four.

It's my mouth, she'd whisper to me, glowing with queenly pride. They take one look and they just *know* – but if you knew what I know, Odette, if you knew that your fiancé's eyes wandered off a long time ago, you wouldn't be laughing any more. Your mouth would be twisted in a new kind of pain, the pain of insecurity, the pus that seeps out as youth drains away.

35

'Two hundred and fifty thousand euros.'

That's what I was offered by a leading cosmetics brand, whose name I can't reveal but begins with a C, to advertise its premium anti-ageing range. The idea had come from Odette – sometimes you really need to stop blabbing, *ma chère*. She'd suggested it to AuDelique, who couldn't afford to engage a model, and one thing led to another: C caught wind of my existence and immediately began dreaming about all the cash they could make.

I was shown a mocked-up advert based on which you were meant to see me applying a cream to my face, in a very soft, delicate light – almost fluffy, like cotton wool. I was supposed to smile just a little, to show how soothing the texture of this particular cream was, with my hair swept back slightly, creating a tousled, semi-styled effect that evoked the world of beauty and skincare. I had bare shoulders and perhaps – only perhaps, it was all up for discussion with me – showed a hint of cleavage. But next to nothing, Betty. Just enough to give you an intimate connection with the character.

There was a headline on the mock-up: *Thirty? No. Forty-five!* The copy alongside explained that, thanks to daily use of this premium skincare range, my wrinkles were now smooth, my cheeks had filled out again, my skin was as finely grained as before, and my youthful looks had returned. It was made clear that the photo hadn't been retouched – you had our word – and that I really did look fifteen years younger than my true age. I had to admit it had a certain elegance.

Of course Odette was elated. You're going to be a star, like Jane Fonda and Sharon Stone – they do ads all over the world. She looked serious for a moment. The only difference, Betty, is that *they*, and I know because I'm in the business and in the business people know everything, well, they're completely doctored in Photo-whatsit. But you're the real deal. You look at least fifteen years younger than you are – even twenty, I'd say! Thanks, Odette, but that's got nothing to do with C's products. That's as may be, she retorted, but two hundred and fifty thousand euros

– read my lips: two-hun-dred-and-fif-ty-thou-sand-euros, can you imagine? It would mean not having to worry about every penny, being able to plan ahead, that's all I've got to say.

She put down her mojito. She looked me straight in the eye.

'And anyway, you could always share it.'

Cue hysterical laughter.

In the end, I turned down the opportunity on the grounds that I found the promise of 'fifteen years younger' a bit of a con. C raised their offer by one hundred thousand euros to overcome my scruples. I thought Odette was going to have a heart attack: and you said no! You went and said no! Good grief, for that money I'd do it, I really would, I'd do it – and totally starkers into the bargain!

Later (that's enough, Odette!), I was contacted by the local broadcaster, France 3 Nord. A journalist from the features team was hoping to meet me, to put together a five-minute profile. She was looking for a fresher approach, perhaps even a bit girly. We'd follow you through your daily routine, go with you to wherever you buy your beauty products. You could talk us through your rituals, how you take care of yourself to stay looking so young. You could tell us about your diet, or whatever sport you're into. I cut her short. You've been told a load of nonsense, I'm terribly sorry. But . . . I . . . Most women, I continued, dream of staying young, but it's a curse, believe me.

And I hung up.

You're all dreaming about what's happened to me. But I'm a circus freak.

36

The sixteenth photo.

A striking image; and to be sure that my portraits would never be contested, Fabrice had had their authenticity and date certified every year by an officer of the court.

The sixteenth photo; sixteen sessions; sixteen faces that should have told the story of my life, my turmoil, my hallelujahs, my despair, my joy, but instead told you nothing at all.

I had become *La Belle Jardinière*, who had appealed to Maman so much, that figure with her everlasting youth. Youth that offers a moment of grace for those who come across it in passing, but is truly terrifying when you reflect on the fact that she's frozen for eternity, as if absent from the world, untainted by wind or fury. You have the impression that no feelings nor any emotions could ever touch her again. Her youth is her prison: she looks so lonely, so perfect, untouched.

I looked at my face, a face that was fifteen years younger than me, and I felt depressed thinking about those women who sacrifice everything for what in truth is a curse – the man I loved had left me because of it. I now attracted only love-struck young men who dreamt of having children with me, of a house and weekends by the sea, or old men who, in my company, wanted to console themselves over the loss of their youth, to give themselves a second chance to be young.

I thought about those women who, like Odette, submit to the knife, disfigure themselves, consent to the stories told by their faces – their own stories – being erased. Purely so they might imagine, for one more year, or maybe two, that they still have the charm to tempt eyes filled with lust. While in fact those eyes reflect nothing more than a primal hunger, which arouses desire, as if desire were only linked to beauty and beauty linked to youth.

I thought about those women, about their struggle to cheat death, because that's the despair that lies at the heart of this. I thought about their losing battle against the first wrinkles, the first loosening of the skin, everything that tells the world that some part of them is beginning to vanish, is irretrievable, their transient bodies, their shame. And I felt like yelling, screaming that only things that don't last have any real value and the threat of this loss is precisely what helps us to survive.

I tore up the sixteenth portrait of myself because I liked the idea of time passing – it shapes our experiences into something unique.

For fifteen years, in these images, nothing had happened at all.

37

He was a little older than my son.

I don't know what I found pleasing in him – his insolence, his boldness or his charm – but I rebuffed him straight away: I'm old enough to be your mother. He broke into a laugh. So, a *maman* who's, what, maybe four, five years older than her son? At least twenty. That's the daftest answer anyone's ever given me, he whispered. I blushed – and it was my embarrassment that told me I would give myself to him.

I put down the books I was about to buy.

'Come, let's go.'

At thirty (almost forty-six), I slept with an attractive young man of twenty-five; my God, I'd forgotten their energy and their eagerness. He had me three times that afternoon. He was inexhaustible, fired up with passion (thanks, Sādhu, for having taught me, and enabled me to master to perfection, the pose known as the Plough, *Halasana*, as without it I'd have been fit for nothing but the paramedics). Finally, when it turned out he needed some time to recover his strength, he came and snuggled up against me, almost sheepishly, and I felt touched.

I always dread the words that come afterwards; making love is all the things you could possibly say and for me the only thing it calls for is silence.

He didn't say a thing.

At thirty (almost forty-six), and more through my casualness than any burning desire, I began a relationship with Xavier S., who was twenty-five, news that got Odette terribly worked up. You've been making such a fuss about not growing old, but just look at the bright side of what's happening to you! she exclaimed. You get to have it off with young guys without people calling you every name under the sun. Ah! You're so lucky, you really are; but let's have it, is he good in bed, this kid of yours?

During the day, Xavier worked for a lawyer, where he drew up deeds for property transactions, while at night, when he wasn't lying beside me, he was working on his novel; a book, he maintained, that sprang from his heart and soul – a vast, sprawling affair, his very own *Under the Volcano*.

His fervour left me spellbound. It reminded me of my own, of being twenty, twenty-five years earlier, at the Pubstore, and that sense of magic. A time, back then, so full of promise that even disappointments left us delighted, even failures left us energised and inspired. We hadn't changed the world – it had changed us. We had simply turned into those little particles of dust that hover in the air, that you sometimes spot in a ray of sunlight.

Whenever Xavier read out passages from his book, violent sentences, or shocking ones, I would let his words float away, like the specks of dust that we are. I didn't try to catch them. They vanished into nothingness. And he would laugh and laugh, and his laughter was clear and bright. He would say, it's beautiful, isn't it, Betty? It's just beautiful. That's blown you away, hasn't it? It's blown you away. And I laughed too, but with a *maman's* laugh, one he could never have suspected. Laughter like arms that open up to become an enchanted place, the place all your journeys unfold.

With him, I constantly felt as though I were about to be unmasked. I loathed him holding my hand or kissing me in the street. I was mortified by the thought of someone noticing our twenty-year gap, pointing, jeering at us – she's screwing one of her son's friends, or maybe even her son, who knows? What a disgrace, the filthy little tart, oh yeah – I'm gonna chuck a load of freezing water over you, you dirty slut. But nothing ever happened – and no one shaved my head, like they did to those women who'd slept with the enemy.

We were a young couple made for each other. When we headed to the coast on some weekends, towards Le

Touquet, Berck or Stella-Plage, people would smile at us, trying to get to know us. Do you play tennis? Could we tempt you to a round of golf? Do your parents own a place in the forest? And occasionally we would go for a drink to Le Westminster or Le Manoir with his friends – I used to choose the same wine as the others so I wouldn't have to take out my glasses.

I discovered young people whose youth was very different to mine, whose youth would come to an end along with the century: boys driving far too fast in their fathers' Range Rovers and girls spending their time texting each other on their new mobile phones, giggling all the while. I was as old as their mothers. And so, one evening, when we were sitting in a group and Xavier put his hand on my knee, trying to stroke the inside of my thigh, I pushed it away discreetly, feeling embarrassed.

Later he made a scene in our room at Le Manoir, a proper little grown-up scene, on the pretext that I'd *made him a laughing stock*. Fuck it, we're a couple. Holy shit, what's the point of that if I can't even touch you? You should've seen Stéphanie's face when she noticed you pushing me away, et cetera. And seeing no reaction, he grabbed the chair nearest to him and sent it flying into the wall, where it smashed into pieces – the violence of men is always born out of misery. I let out a muffled cry; he calmed down at once and came closer to me, shaking, like a puppy afraid of getting a smack. Please forgive me, Betty, I'm sorry. And I – who had a son barely any younger than him, who knew all about boys and their fits of anger, their fiery spirit – I took him in my arms. I know, Xavier, you love me – and often loving someone means being alone.

38

At thirty (forty-six plus), my medical tests confirmed their positive opinion of my state of health.

My insides were growing old precisely as they should. Oxidation was degrading my tissues, while the deterioration of my mitochondria couldn't have looked any better and – in common with everyone else – had lowered energy levels in my cells. My rate of decrease of methylation was perfect. And my long-sightedness was increasing correctly, having reached one and a half dioptres. On the other hand, my telomeres were not getting any shorter. Those, explained Hagop Haytayan, are what control the regeneration of your skin – hence its baby-soft texture, my complexion being similar to a young girl's, my still being thirty every morning, the jealous gaze of other women and the bewitched look on men's faces.

Papa's tests were more worrying. The ageing process was speeding up and, despite it being a normal part of life, the doctors were astonished that it should be accelerating quite so fast. According to Françoise, the dark Long John Silver had surfaced again: Papa was turning nasty – an unpredictable, quick-tempered child, in the mutilated body of a giant. Sometimes I'll even hide his fake leg and his crutches, just to pin him down in that vile poo-coloured chair of his, she confided in me one day. Has he ever harmed you, Françoise? She cast her eyes down and I knew what the answer was.

It was only when I came to visit that Papa was calm. He would look at me wearing that mild-mannered, almost idiotic expression found in people who don't know any-thing about the world, or the fury of men. He was amiable and spoke to me in an elegant voice, as you might pick up an elegant quill to write. I'm so happy you're here, so happy you're home. I've been waiting for you all day with Jeanne. Who's Jeanne? Our daughter. We've been watching TV. Is it cold outside? Your cheeks are all red and the wind's messed up your hair.

Then each time Françoise took refuge in her room, or when I said goodbye, tears fell from her eyes. I liked Françoise. I liked her heart of gold and her patience – she never complained. Whenever I came, she would make the most of it by going out, meeting up with a few ex-saleswomen from Le Chat Noir, enjoying *macarons* at Méert, or waffles made with Madagascan vanilla, and perhaps a cup of Joséphine tea – rediscovering the pleasant taste of the world.

A few weeks later, she put Papa in a nursing home.

'Now, I'd like to feel young again,' she said. 'To be as lucky as you.'

'It's no picnic being like me, Françoise. People look at me but it's not me they see. Just an anomaly. An illusion.'

'Maybe, but at least I'd feel beautiful.'

'You are.'

'No, Betty. Beautiful is when a man hasn't forgotten who you are.'

39

At thirty (forty-seven), Xavier dropped the final full stop into his novel and our relationship.

He'd seen me coming out of my studio in the company of another young man: we were laughing and joking, I had stroked one of his cheeks and kissed the other, and Xavier had convinced himself that I was having an affair with *this guy*. He said some really mean things, as men always do when they're scared. I didn't defend myself. I didn't tell him it was in fact my son, Sébastien, with whom I'd just had lunch, as I had done every Tuesday since his father left. Because you don't have a son of twenty-two when you only look thirty yourself, because the very idea is beyond belief – even for a young writer who's just completed *a book that sprang from his heart and soul*.

At forty-seven, since I only looked thirty and since, in any case, I was thirty in the eyes of the world, I began to hang around certain hotel bars in the late afternoon: the Bellevue, the Couvent des Minimes, L'Hermitage Gantois. I read. I waited. I quivered with anticipation. I wanted to be like women of my age who dream of being thirty again, of being devoured by men, of hearing once more the distinctive language of desire and knowing it's meant for them. I dreamt of saying yes, yes this seat's free, yes I'll have the same, no, I'm not waiting for anyone, and savouring the effect five words can have on a man's appetite. And then laughing, to reassure him, before going up to his room, slapping any old name on myself, letting him touch me, explore me, gaze at me, daring to use vulgar words when he took me, daring to act all precious.

At thirty (forty-seven), I had the pleasure of several late-afternoon lovers.

But not one could discover within me what my husband had already found.

40

The eighteenth photo.

The same pearly backdrop. The same light. The same white blouse, worn for the eighteenth time. The same hairstyle. The same slightly open lips. Peggy Daniels. A miracle, more or less the same every year, repeating itself, bizarre and yet fascinating too.

At forty-seven, I still didn't have a single frown line and none on my forehead. No crow's feet or laughter lines.

No marionette lines nor any on my décolletage – none whatsoever. Not a single grey hair, no rings under my eyes. I was as hopelessly thirty as you could ever be.

Fabrice showed me the thirty-eighth image of his first model. Forty-nine and still as handsome – he had something of an Italian actor about him.

The little girl he'd started photographing in her sleep at the age of two was now sixteen; and yes, he would still wait until she'd fallen asleep before taking a picture. These were peculiar images, tinged with melancholy: Millais' *Ophelia*, two lines by Rimbaud – *For a thousand years and more, sad Ophelia / Has drifted by, a white ghost, on the long, black river.*

On Time would be an astounding book. A book about how we gradually fade away.

There was also the fifteenth portrait of a man. A thousand francs each time! Well, a hundred and fifty euros now, said Fabrice, correcting himself. But he's here every year, the guy who's tattooed all over, the one I met in a bar when he was just out of prison. His face was shrivelled and wrinkled, as if he were eating himself from the inside.

And the fifteenth photo of the woman who had looked so much like a youthful Odette; she had now lost her milky-white cheeks and all of her promise.

We exchanged glances. We both knew.

He then showed me a new portrait: a pale Odette, Botticelli-esque, strawberry blonde, a graceful young woman of twenty or so. I asked him why he still hadn't left his fiancée. I'm going to, her name's Sybille. Odette's going to die of loneliness, I muttered. No, she's made of stronger stuff. No woman is strong when she's growing old, Fabrice, she's terrified, that's all. And if you leave her because you're looking for what she once was in someone else, you'll kill her.

41

One night, a year later.

    Scattered around me, on the bed, are Fabrice's nineteen photos. My face, nineteen times over. Nineteen times the pearly-white backdrop, my lips slightly open, my hair down. Nineteen times the same image, apart from the year the shot was taken, marked in black felt tip bottom right. Nineteen sessions.

My fingers brush gently over eyes made of paper,

cheeks, mouths that refuse to smile. My fingers twitch nervously. I'm sweating. My heart's racing. There's something horrifying about this series and yet sublime at the same time. Something everlasting. A permanence that defies all comprehension. And although it's the dead of night, I feverishly dial the number for Hagop Haytayan. He answers almost immediately, his voice perfectly clear – a very calm *hello?* He recognises me at once.

Doctor, do you think that . . . My words – hideous, extraordinary words – stick in my throat. That . . . That I might be immortal? No, Betty, he whispers, no. You'll die young, that's all. I mean, of old age.

But young.

42

Long John Silver occupied a room at Notre Dame de la Treille in Valenciennes, in a former *hôtel particulier* that had belonged to a family of wealthy cloth merchants, the Serrets, for a long time.

The medicines had finally got the better of his temper and when we paid him a visit, he was subdued, almost in a world of his own – he's in a daze, said Françoise. We spent an hour with him. Françoise thanked him for the moments of grace he had given her – like Italy, when she'd been sick with worry because of Michel, like the kir he would make out of loyalty to my mother, like their little trips out to Bray-Dunes and Zuydcoote. He spoke very little, barely even about what he was eating – it's too salty – or watching on TV – it's stuck on Channel 2. Sometimes he scrutinised me out of the corner of his eye before nodding gently and sighing, hissing Maman's name ten, twenty, a hundred times.

Françoise didn't cry any more.

On the way back, we stopped off in Petite-Forêt; a coffee, a *tartelette* at Flunch. We sat in silence for a long time, reluctant to talk about him, or to put the destruction we had witnessed into words. For the second time in her life, Françoise had been abandoned for a younger woman, but this time her rival was a ghost – and there's nothing you can do about them.

She studied me with her gentle eyes. Are you happy, Betty? I glanced down for a second. Then I opened up about my joy and my distress at not growing old. I talked about my childish excitement at finding each morning that nothing about my face had changed. At knowing that people would smile at me the same way in the street, as if paying me compliments. That men would still come up to me in hotels – can I get you the same again? I'm too shy to tell you how stunning you are. Have you seen that *American Beauty* everyone's talking about? Have you read the latest book to win the Goncourt? You're as graceful as a portrait by Raphael. I recalled what I'd once believed when I was younger, namely that happiness was to be found in things that lasted for ever, but I was wrong, Françoise. Staying the same is terrifying.

My husband had left me because nothing about me had altered, because my appearance was a lie, because it no longer told our story, because my permanence reflected his own finite existence.

I talked about my bitterness at having been a woman of thirty for more than eighteen years, at seeing the world changing around me without feeling part of it. I touched on fears yet to come: before long my son will be my age, then he'll start to look older than me. He'll call me by my name. I'll become a sister, a friend. I shall never again be his *maman*.

I talked about my mother, whom I would dearly have loved to see growing old, with pretty wrinkles tracing laughter and delight across her face, as fine as calligraphy, charting her battles and her anguish. I would have loved to watch her gliding through time like a bird across the sky, because a mother who's no longer getting old, who's stopped in her tracks, is like the child she's left behind, a child who'll never grow any more. So whether I'm happy or not, I'm not sure, Françoise, but I have been. I have been, with André.

You know, I'm soon going to be seventy-three, she said, and I've been so happy, Betty, so happy you've been my daughter, and part of my life, for so long. You've been my joy, my hope when Michel was doing all that horrid stuff. The shame's almost killed me, but thanks to you I'm still here. I've managed to keep going. I've still managed to be a *maman*. I've kept my dignity. And I'm also grateful to Paule, your *maman*, who was certainly a brave woman since I know her pain – your *papa*'s fits of anger, the insanity of men who don't love themselves any more.

I felt like crying. I placed my hand on hers.

I'm also pleased things don't last for ever – you know, that they come to an end, because that ending brings with it something that kills us but sets us free too. And I need that freedom now, Betty.

Yet another person I loved who was leaving me.

43

The photo was tucked away, surrounded by others, on the gossip page of an international interiors magazine – we received a lot of magazines at La Redoute, we called it 'the info'. It showed André along with an attractive woman of the same age, a Swedish Jacqueline Bisset (she wasn't short on looks), during a private viewing at Kompanihuset, in Malmö, Sweden. The caption, in English, read: *Famous French designer, André Delattre, with his fiancée,*

Lena Åberg, at the preview for his new furniture collection.

It was the French word in the caption that hurt the most.

At thirty (forty-nine), I saw my husband looking happy on another woman's arm, but I didn't go to pieces.

Shortly after, I celebrated my son's twenty-fifth birthday with him during a long, glorious weekend in Paris: Japanese restaurants on Rue Sainte-Anne; the Grande Galerie of the Louvre, Room 710, *La Belle Jardinière*. I told him about the *maman* he had never known, other than through a Polaroid. I told him about how moved she had been in front of this painting by Raphael, a beauty that seemed slightly lost, time slipping past, time that refused to take hold, the clamour and clatter that left no mark. Like on you, he said. Like on me, Sébastien, that's right. And he took me in his arms, this huge strapping lad who was taller than me, even taller than his father now.

He whispered in my ear that he loved me just as I was, that I was the prettiest *maman* of all. And since I was deeply touched, and he could foresee embarrassing tears, he laughed and added that everything might change one of these days. That I would probably wake up one morning as a very old woman, mega-old in fact, as wrinkly as a rotten apple, smelling of mothballs and mould. And my laughter blended with his until people thought we were young lovers; then the magic flew away and sorrow, like ashes, rained down on us once more.

In the train on the way back from Paris, Sébastien told me he'd gone to see his father in Sweden a few weeks earlier and that he'd met Lena. So? I asked. Well, nothing much, really. She's head over heels and Papa's pretty laid-back with her. Oh. But he mostly talked about you. And? And I think that . . . What? Well, he talked about you both a lot, about how you two first met. I'd no idea he'd chatted you up in the street. I smiled. So? Nothing, I just found it touching when he talked about it. But he's getting married? But he's getting married and I'm not going to their wedding, Maman, I swear. Let's go and have a drink in the buffet car, shall we, Sébastien?

The following day, I was given another slap in the face.

44

'You're being made redundant.'

'Sorry?'

'Redundant. We're letting you go.'

'I know what it means. Why?'

'We're in the twenty-first century, Betty. The world's moved on. The mail order business, it's all changed. We're in the digital age now. Everything's going to be done by computers.'

'Maybe, but a computer's not going to write my copy for me.'

'You'd be surprised. Recently, a computer beat a man at chess. And not just anyone. Kasparov.'

'That's maths. But I'm talking words.'

'Well, we're not here to – at least, yes, but . . . I'm sorry, Betty, really sorry.'

'And my nineteen years' service?'

'You're not the only one. It's part of a restructuring plan. Mail order's changing, so the costs need to flex accordingly.'

'What, so computers end up writing instead of us?'

'Exactly. And because the catalogue's far too expensive. The cost of paper . . . and transport. In future, we're going to offer our products online. People will think it's great fun. It'll be very efficient, you'll see.'

'I'll see nothing of the sort. I'm fifty. You know full well that when you're fifty, you're too old for the job market, you're a fossil. Your dustbin's basically a letter box for our CVs.'

'Er, you're fifty?'

'It's there, in your file.'

'Ah. Ah, yes. Oh, look, so it is. But . . .'

'But what?'

'It's very odd, Betty. You don't look it at all. I could have sworn you were thirty and given you're so . . . attract-ive, I'd have thought you'd find work very easily.'

'That's pretty shocking, if that's what you're thinking. And anyhow, it's what a guy would think, and a bloody dickhead at that. It's no wonder that once they're past a certain age, women start hating themselves.'

The young director of human resources settled back into her massive leather director-of-human-resources arm-chair, which let out a squeak, and eyed me up and down for a few seconds – as you might, I guess, scan a model in a fashion magazine – with a sort of jealousy mixed with irritation. Then her lips curved into a smile. A wolf at the kill.

'No. Seriously, Betty, you can't be fifty. Is this a joke? A typo?'

'Listen, I need glasses to read small print. My knees hurt when it's cold, and my hands too. I'm finding it harder and harder to fall asleep, I'm out of breath climbing more than four floors and I've already had the infinite pleasure of the post-menopause – so no, I don't think I'm a typo.'

45

I strip naked.

I examine my face in the bathroom mirror. It looks like Maman's, just before the Ford Taunus. It's identical to the photo Fabrice took more than twenty years ago.

I look at my mouth, my eyes and my neck. My body's as firm as ever. You wouldn't know that becoming a mother had once sliced it in two.

I look at my hands. Hands that don't shake. The skin

on my wrist, so very fine, at the spot where you'd cut it when you didn't love yourself any more, or no longer loved your life.

I look at the tears now streaming down my cheeks.

I turn off the light. I am in the dark and I wait.

Then I put the light back on and the face is still there. The dark once more. Light. A face in the mirror, like in a Polaroid or an oil painting on wood, one that time has forgotten.

I turn off the light again.

My nails dig in like claws and the tears on my cheeks feel warm. Sticky.

Red paint trickles down the picture in the darkness.

46

Fabrice left Odette as winter came to an end and moved in with the woman who looked like her but was as young as spring.

And as for me, at thirty (fifty-one), I was, in professional terms, only fit for the scrapheap.

I spent two days at Odette's place. She cried her eyes out – I cried as well – and she drank a lot. Far too much. Getting drunk made her cry even more, or burst out laughing, for no reason at all, and her words spewed out in a muddle. It's 'cos you're so frigging old, that's for sure, *ma chère*. You're buggered, y'know. On the other hand, though, look at that face of yours . . . But hey, you've got a cat now, have you? No? I really thought so, yeah really, 'cos of your face, y'see, that's what I thought.

And she broke down again. Her mascara began to run, scrawling brambly lines down her cheeks. Ooh, they *do* look nasty, those scratches you've got. And look at me, look at my old face, Betty. It's beastly too. I so wanted to stay looking beautiful for him, but there you go. Fucking hell, what a prick! Why the fuck do they all want cute little girls? It's not like their cunts are fountains of youth, not far as I know. And laughter and tears merged with each other.

So it's a guy, then – those scratches, you've got yourself a man, is that it? One of those fiery types. No, Odette, I don't have a man. I'm sixty, she went on, and now my guy's dumped me for some little slut who's twenty. What a bastard. And anyhow, he's getting more handsome the older he gets, the bloody arsehole. He's even better-looking than he was before. They're all a pile of shit, guys. Yep, the whole damn lot, even your man. See! Now he's chucking *you* out *because* you're twenty. Thirty, Odette. Same difference, they're like kids, always after what they've not got. Oh, fuck, my head hurts.

On the second day, her eyes still swollen and her mouth feeling claggy, she finally hauled herself off the sofa. I'm going to have a shower, I'm absolutely stinking, and then I'm off to screw a few lads, Betty. Some young guys, some twenty-year-olds. I'll show 'em just what an old woman's good at. What a *princess* can do.

And she collapsed into tears.

A few months later, Michel came out of jail where he'd been for seventeen years. Françoise went to pick him up from Poissy Central Prison. His hair had turned white all over and he had the broken frame of an old man – even though we were the same age, or at least were born in the same year. He was missing some teeth and perhaps even his tongue, because he didn't speak. Not a word.

Françoise drove him to the house she'd bought with Papa when she had been his crutch, his right leg, back when he knew how to comfort her. She showed her son the well-stocked fridge and his room. Here are your sheets and towels, and some new clothes. In here you've got a toothbrush, toothpaste, soap. In the living room, the TV, the buttons on the remotes for the various devices. In the kitchen, she made him a sandwich with chocolate spread, like the ones she remembered him loving so much, before the motorbikes, the darkness and the acts of pure evil.

She slid a biscuit tin towards him, with some cash inside. She didn't utter a single word either. She didn't ask for anything, neither an explanation nor for him to beg forgiveness. And then, when she saw Michel reach for the chocolate *tartine* from his childhood, that's when she got up, put the chair back under the table, without scraping the legs, picked up her coat and her bag, and went out.

That was the day Françoise vanished from our lives.

47

At thirty (fifty-two), after three months' training in the craft of upholstery, specialising in refurbishing chairs, armchairs and sofas, I opened a workshop, Sitting Pretty, in a lovely cobbled courtyard on Rue de la Halloterie. I put out some flowers, a table and three chairs; the neighbours would drop in for a cup of tea in the mornings, or a glass of white wine in the evenings, and it wasn't long before I had enough work to keep my hands busy and my days fully occupied.

I stocked a range of vintage upholstery fabrics – Pierre Frey, Lelièvre and Francesca Laubscher, who'd previously been at Canovas – that enthralled my clients. When the weather was pleasant, I would be outside, pinking the edges of material, back tacking a seat cover or fixing some webbing while the neighbours looked on, spellbound. They said how good it was to see a young woman going into this line of work, and I smiled at the thought of giving furniture a new lease of life. One day, a customer asked me what I'd done before becoming an upholsterer and I replied without thinking twice: a primary school teacher for four years, then a *maman*, then a copywriter for La Redoute for twenty years. She sparkled with laughter: you're not just talented, you know, you're a total scream!

Then, one lunchtime, I saw André crossing the courtyard.

48

We hadn't seen each other for ten months.

The last time had been in June. A lunch on the terrace – just like before, when the future still lay ahead, when we thought we'd live through a whole century together, until one day we became a little old couple whose beauty and tenderness had rubbed off on each other. Sébastien had joined us for dessert and for an hour we'd been a family once more. He and André were talking man-type stuff – some new Japanese make of hybrid car, which had apparently been a sensation in a motor race, won by a Spanish driver, I think – and I was carried away. I imagined them again, twenty years earlier, exchanging the words for parts of a tree, *crown, bark, sapwood*, or the names of the winds, *white squall, galerne, aquilo*. Or setting off to go fishing in the stream at Sainghin, then coming home with a great big sole bought at the fishmonger's. And me being astounded by their catch and Sébastien laughing and laughing, and it seemed that nothing could ever come between us. Then our son headed back to Amsterdam where he worked. André and I shared one last coffee and went our separate ways.

I saw him crossing the courtyard that day and my heart leapt as it had before. I was eighteen again – which, in a sense, was the root of the problem – and I ran towards him. He threw his arms around me and sent us spinning around on ourselves before bringing us to a standstill. We lingered in each other's arms for a few long seconds and one of the local residents, busy watering her azaleas and hibiscuses, called out: what a lucky *papa*, having a daughter like you! André gently loosened his grip. We looked at each other and laughed. At last.

I opened a bottle of white wine and we had our aperitif right there, on my little iron table, in the flower-filled square. You seem well settled here, I'm really happy for you. You can see I'm into armchairs and chairs, like you. He raised his glass in a toast. I can see that, but in your case, you're mending them, you're breathing life back into them. But you too, André – you breathe life into things. Your hands have that touch of genius.

He let out a long sigh. I'm giving up my design work. But . . . Let me explain, Betty. I'm giving up because I've got less and less freedom. It's the company I design for. They're determined to make me sign up with Ikea – it's a nice fat contract, four collections over two years, but an impossible list of specifications, budgets slashed to the bare bones. And you, you like leaving things to chance, I know. You like changing direction according to the wind. He smiled, with that smile I loved so much. You know me so well, Betty. I haven't forgotten you, André. And anyway, you're just like your parents: things need to come from the heart, not the head. And stop looking at me with those eyes! Sorry? Gene Kelly. And we laughed again, and it felt good.

I dashed off to buy some cheeses, grapes and a *pain aux noix*, and we picnicked in the courtyard. I studied him closely. His salt-and-pepper hair. Two attractive folds running down his cheeks when he smiled. He was nearing sixty – he wore his age well – and even if he'd never been the most handsome of boys, nor the worst-looking either, the years had lent him an incredible charm. Disconcerting and yet alluring.

Later, he told me that his engagement to Lena had been – how can I put this? – put on hold. No, broken off. We had some major disagreements about the basics in life (here's hoping, Maman, that he didn't hear my little sigh of relief). He had returned to France for good around six months earlier and bought what was once a farmhouse, close to the farm where he'd grown up. We talked about Renée, his *maman*, who was now eighty-five, still living in the south of France. She'd been in a home for the elderly for several months – all she does is sit and wait. She's pining for her lost youth; you can't imagine how frightened she is.

Then I placed my hand on his and he made no attempt to pull it back. Yes, I know, but it's not youth that disappears, André, it's people. As we grow old, death begins to peek through in our faces. We know we'll soon be rubbed out like chalk. We're terrified by the thought of a world still turning without us. He smiled and I fell silent.

Enough of that. Let's talk about the living, Betty. Happy things. Hey! Guess what? I'm about to join the team at 'The Tree House'. It's an amazing project – it's led by Alain Laurens. He's a terrific guy – *it's the tree itself that wraps around each house, deciding its precise position and design; and each one is installed without chopping a single branch, or hammering a single nail into the living wood.* I was delighted for him.

Then he asked me how I was. I'm living on my own, I replied. I have met a few guys, but things are all screwed up these days: the young ones want to settle down, to have kids, and the older ones simply want someone young. I'm still close to Odette. She'll never get over Fabrice leaving. We'll probably go to Portugal this summer, the two of us, to a holiday club in Albufeira. I've been alone all this time, André. Lonely.

As lonely as the damned.

Later that afternoon, even though he was meant to leave, we held each other in a long embrace. In the window of my workshop I saw our reflections, our faces. I saw the thirty years that divided us from each other.

A wasted life.

49

A s soon as the film began, one of the audience suc-
cumbed to an uncontrollable fit of the giggles that,
for an hour and a half, swept through the entire auditor-
ium – and I've never found out whether it was *Little Miss
Sunshine* that was so hilarious or this man's hysterical
laughter.

In 2006, a chubby little girl from Albuquerque in New
Mexico dreamt of winning a beauty pageant – and the

thing I'd been dreading loomed on the horizon.

Two years later, I was the same age as my son.

The year after, he was older than me.

At thirty (almost fifty-six), Sébastien told me he wanted to introduce me to Saga. He showed me a few photos: a tall, blonde girl who worked with him at the Consulate General of France in Amsterdam and with whom he wanted to spend his life, to eat organic food and have blond children, a yellow Labrador and an electric car some day. Yes, Saga was the one; the girl with whom he dreamt of slowly growing old, of living through an entire century to become – in time – a little old couple, deeply in love, holding each other's hands, et cetera.

He asked me to help him choose an engagement ring. I took him to Lepage, on Rue de la Bourse – which made me think of André, thirty-two years earlier, on bended knee on the covered bridge straddling the Bouzanne, and my tears when I'd said yes. We looked at the rings in the window, the solitaires. That one's magnificent! exclaimed my son. Then he saw the price. Well, maybe not as magnificent as all that. In fact, oh, look, over there, that blue diamond. It's an aquamarine, Sébastien; he'd become a child again, the boy I'd watched growing up, awestruck by everything.

A salesman came out of the shop and invited us to come in. You make such a lovely couple, he observed with sincerity, and my son was about to put him right, but I was quicker off the mark. Thank you. Thanks very much. He showed us some engagement rings that I slipped on my finger, surprised, delighted, letting out a few little gasps of *oh!* which Sébastien found charming. He laughed, kissing my neck every now and then, or my hand, like a fervent adolescent dressed up as a man – my man, my fiancé.

So when are you planning to have the wedding? ventured the salesman. Next spring, said Sébastien, playing along. Do you know what colour the dress will be? That might help with choosing the stone. No, no, we haven't found one yet, but it'll be all white, like Elaine's in *The Graduate*, with embroidery! Then I put the last ring back. We'll have a think about it. I held my son's hand, like a bouquet, like a fiancée, and we went out into the street hand in hand, into the crowds of passers-by – *such a lovely young couple.*

My heart was pounding. My son's eyes were shining. We didn't speak; it felt unreal. I dragged him towards the Old Stock Exchange market, with its second-hand booksellers and scattering of chess players. A couple, in their forties, looked at us enviously. I was twenty-five again, radiant, with long, pale legs, the same smile I'd had when André had come up to me, a few streets away.

I stopped suddenly and moved closer to my son. I caressed his face, both the man and the child, his cheeks, his eyelids, his lips, like a *maman* or a young girl, like his betrothed. I remained like this for several long minutes, somewhere on the edge of things I was losing and finding at the same time. He caught hold of my fingers, brought them up to his mouth, kissed them one by one, then let them go as if releasing a baby bird from the palm of his hand. I knew he was saying farewell to childhood. And I felt happy, for an instant, at having been all the women in his life.

But children can sometimes be cruel, almost despite

themselves, and awaken us with brutal words: I can't introduce you as my mother, there's just no way. I'm sorry, Maman.

We let go of each other's hand and our bodies moved apart. We left the calm and the cool air of the inner courtyard at the Old Stock Exchange and returned to the violence of the world, to people rushing past, and cars. Disharmony.

He introduced me as his cousin.

I knew he wouldn't say *mulieris est*, this is my mother, this is the woman who brought me into this life, she's very special indeed. The woman who loved me from the very first day, from the very first second, who was afraid and cold for me when I was afraid and cold. The woman who produced the man that I am from her belly, taller than his father now. The man who loves you today, Saga, and is about to take you as his wife. And even though I knew all that, I still felt like crying and running away; but I neither cried nor ran away, because a *maman* must remain standing under the weight of sorrow and shame and tears.

Mothers learn they are going to die from their sons.

We had a hot chocolate at L'Impertinente and shared a *tarte aux fruits*. Yet I dreamt of being elsewhere, because I was no longer a *maman*, no longer a wife, nothing at all. Nothing but a pretty cousin aged thirty – single, an upholsterer, she's really talented, explained my son. She's just restored an entire *causeuse*, also known as a *tête-à-tête*. You'd call it a courting sofa, Saga. But I wasn't mad with him, any more than I'd been mad with my husband when, in the car on the way back from Paris, he'd announced he was leaving.

My everlasting youth was a punishment.

A few months later, André and I travelled together to attend our son's wedding in Holland.

Sitting in the high-speed train, I longed to hold his hand. To tell him I loved him. That I had missed him every day, every night, for more than thirteen years. That I'd lost a baby, on the tenth of May 1981, while he'd been away renovating a timber frame in Saint-Denis-d'Anjou, while half of France was singing in hope and the other was busy stashing away its silver.

He told me that our son was the apple of his father's eye, and he thanked me for that.

The celebrations took place at the Waldorf Astoria, *ma chère*, six seventeenth-century palaces strung alongside the Herengracht canal, like pearls around the neck of a beautiful woman. It was a joyful evening and a great success. André and I were at the same table, with eight other guests. Foie gras and yuzu cream, Zeeland flat oysters – I was dining on perfume. Later it was time for dancing, a time for the young ones. André managed to sneak off. I was about to do the same, when a lad put out his hand and stopped me: tall, blond, Dutch, attractive. It's not time for pretty young cousins to go to bed, he said, in English. Unless it's with me, he added, with no pretention, no sense of urgency, almost with a charming sense of tact.

And that night, the pretty young cousin of fifty-five slipped away with the bride's young brother.

So there you have it. My dream life.

50

The cosmetic surgeon stared at me for a long time and then, in a voice that seemed barely a whisper:

'Are you sure?'

'Yes.'

He'd been asked for everything and he'd seen all there was to see.

Women of fifty-seven, sixty, seventy, oh yes, and even younger, thirty-five, sometimes thirty and even nineteen one time – can you imagine, *nineteen*?

But what you've asked for now, believe me, I've never, ever had anyone ask for *that* before, never, not in my wildest dreams.

Oh my God.

Sixty-Three

51

Here's the thirty-fourth photograph.

I am standing, as always. In front of the pearly-white backdrop. The light is both harsh and elegant. My hair, which I've dyed grey, is down, the collar of my white blouse is open, two buttons undone, you can see the skin on my neck, now drooping a little. I'm trying not to smile, keeping my lips slightly open, two millimetres or so. You can make out tiny wrinkles and scars, and fine scratches, around my mouth and eyes, and more defined creases on my forehead. My frown lines and marionette lines are both visible. My cheeks are sagging slightly more than before. My eyelids are heavier and faint little bags have appeared below my eyes, making the skin there darker. Minute spots of rust have appeared on my hands. As if someone's hammered in upholstery nails. The skin on my arms has lost its firmness and feels loose.

Try not to smile, says Fabrice for the thirty-fourth time. Because I can't help smiling. Because I'm happy. Because I'm sixty-three. You're beautiful, says the photographer. And we can finally see the signs of pain and joy on your face – I think they're superb, Betty. They tell your story. Your incredible story. Try not to smile; and click, flash, a shimmer of stars in my eyes, the photo's been taken. That's amazing. I think my book's ready now. Thank you, Betty, thank you so much.

52

When the estate agent came to put the 'Lease For Sale' sign on the window of Sitting Pretty, Yvonne, the neighbour who always took great care of her flowers, came running over, panic-stricken. What's the matter? What's going on? She examined me closely, clearly taken aback: oh, you, you're Betty's *maman*, has something happened? I smiled, no, nothing's happened to her, she simply decided to leave. She wanted a different kind of life, closer to her true self, the kind she's always dreamt about. Oh, what a pity, muttered the gardener, what a pity. She was ever so kind. It was such a pleasure having a young lady here with us. Please do ask her to keep in touch. I promise; and I couldn't help putting my arms around her – she asked me to give you a hug. Really? replied Yvonne, suddenly wide-eyed with wonder, like a little girl in a toy shop. Yes, really, she was very fond of you; and then I was gone.

At Lille Flandres station, I hired a quiet, comfortable car; then I left the city and took the A1 autoroute, heading towards Paris. Bach, on Radio Classique; his adaptation of a piece by Alessandro Marcello, a haunting adagio, the sound of grace. Kilometres rolled by peacefully. I smiled. I smiled just as I'd smiled at eighteen, while walking alone, while climbing aboard the city tram, just as when André had come up to me and asked why I was smiling.

I shall go and see my son and Saga. I'll explain to them that I'd lost my bearings and needed time to find my way back – an entire lifetime, in fact. That I'm his *maman* and not his cousin. That my arms are branches, sturdy branches that will never grow tired, a place to cling to on stormy days, a place to tether lonely clouds and dreams.

I'll teach my charming daughter-in-law how to make *goyère* and a roast – *rare, Saga, rare, otherwise it's tough as old boots* – flavoured with bay leaves and thyme, sprinkled with finely chopped garlic, and a tart using speculoos biscuits. I'll confess that I used to be called Martine and Betty's the name I adopted later, after surviving the pain. I'll confess to my son one evening that he had a little brother or sister, who slipped out of my belly one jubilant night, whom my hands weren't able to catch but whom I still talk to, after dark, from time to time, telling them about their big brother here on Earth. I'll be a kind-hearted, affectionate grandmother, someone who's always there for you. I shall find the recipe for the best hot chocolate in the world and when my grandchildren come to visit, I'll mark their height on their bedroom doorposts.

I drove past Paris. The ring road. The barbaric way some people drive. Gentilly. Chevilly-Larue. The ugliness of my surroundings. Grey, filthy. The shocking taste some men have. Caccini's 'Ave Maria' in the passenger compartment. I'll tell them about my mother, about the painting by Raphael. I'll tell them about the ochre Ford Taunus, the speed, the rush of air, like a hurricane, then a dull thud and suddenly silence – her body mown down in a moment of pure joy, tossed fifteen metres away, torn apart. I'll talk about my desire to keep her close to me ever since, my helplessness and my sorrow. I'll tell them about Long John Silver, and if he's still alive then perhaps I'll take them to see him, to show them they're the grandchildren of so much strength, and so much suffering, to prove you can survive the heat of the fire.

I stopped to fill up. To drink some insipid tea. To eat something soft and squishy. Then I took to the road again. Lorries forming an endless queue, like a monstrous serpent. The sun began to disappear – an orange slipping from a tree, in slow motion. Car headlights, like festive paper lanterns. After Lyon, Valence, Montélimar. Exit: Avignon South.

I remembered I'd promised myself I'd go to the festival one summer and I'd never been – there's always some excuse for not keeping your own word. Route Nationale 7.

By night. Magical names. Apt. Jonquerettes. L'Isle-sur-la-Sorgue. I found a room at the Hôtel Les Névons and collapsed into bed, exhausted.

In the morning, I had breakfast by the river. Three children laughed as they threw pebbles at the mallards. An hour when time stood still. A handsome old lady sat on her own, in the shade of some chestnut trees. Two English men nodded at me in greeting. I explored the village, known as the Venice of the Comtat. Waterwheels. Quays. Churches and chapels. Carpet mills. Fishermen. Their astonishing little boats called *nègo-chin* – literally 'drown-dog', heaven knows why. And antiques, of course.

Then I was back on the road. Cavaillon. Les Vignères. Bonnieux, at last. A spectacular view of the Petit Luberon and, to the north, the plateaux of the Vaucluse Mountains. It was almost midday. I had to ask the way to Alain Laurens' house several times. Ah, Tarzan! exclaimed a man, chuckling. He's bananas, y'know. He'll be leaping around in a tree and if not, um, you'll find him at home. He'll be with his work pals, um, second on the left, at the iron cross. You can't miss it, m'dame, oh no.

The men and two women were sitting at a table in the garden, in the shade. They were chatting loudly, laughing, drinking rosé, sharing a meal of dark bread, cheese, ham and fruit. Their faces beamed with joy, eyes sparkling with sunlight. Their hands were broad and strong, and could recognise white ash, or Douglas fir, or amboyna burr purely by touch alone.

I approached slowly, my hand shielding my eyes from the sun. I was trembling even though it was warm. A man pointed at me, then others turned to look in my direction.

One of them sat transfixed. Then his hand appeared to come back to life and he laid his fork down on his plate. He rose to his feet and it seemed he was shaking as much as I was. He took a few hesitant steps. He stopped. Two more steps. Then he smiled. His entire body seemed to be smiling. Flowering. Even his sad Gene Kelly eyes were smiling.

And so, at sixty-three, I started running like a madwoman and threw myself into the arms of the love of my life.

Old age is a victory in itself.

Acknowledgements

To Elsa Misson and Eva Bredin, whose magical touch can make a book fly.

To Kirsty Dunseath and Federico Andornino, for embracing my words with such verve and flair.

To Vineet Lal, for giving those words a new land to call home.

To Dana, with whom I shall never fear growing old.

Read on for an excerpt from
The List of My Desires . . .

The international bestselling sensation

*Money can buy you freedom.
But what about happiness?*

We're always telling ourselves lies.

For instance, I know I'm not pretty. I don't have blue eyes, the kind in which men gaze at their own reflection, eyes in which they want to drown so that I'll dive in to rescue them. I don't have the figure of a model, I'm more the cuddly sort – well . . . plump. The sort who takes up a seat and a half. A man of medium height won't be able to get his arms all the way round me. I don't move with the grace of a woman to whom men whisper sweet nothings, punctuated by sighs . . . no, not me. I get brief, forthright comments. The bare bones of desire, nothing to embellish them, no comfortable padding.

I know all that.

All the same, when Jo isn't home I sometimes go up to our bedroom and stand in front of the long mirror in our wardrobe – I must remind Jo to fix it to the wall before it squashes me flat one of these days while I'm in the midst of my *contemplation*.

Then I close my eyes and I undress, gently, the way no one has ever undressed me. I always feel a little cold; I shiver. When I'm entirely naked, I wait a little while before opening my eyes. I enjoy that moment. My mind wanders. I dream. I imagine the beautiful paintings of languid bodies in the art books that used to lie around my parents' house, and later I think of the more graphic bodies you see pictured in magazines.

Then I gently open my eyes, as if lifting the lids in slow motion.

I look at my body, my black eyes, my small breasts, my plump spare tyre, my forest of black hair, I think I look beautiful, and I swear that, in that moment, I really *am* beautiful, very beautiful even.

My beauty makes me profoundly happy. Tremendously strong.

It makes me forget unpleasant things. The haberdashery shop, which is quite boring.

The chit-chat of Danièle and Françoise, the twins who run the Coiff'Esthétique hair salon next door to my shop, and their obsession with playing the lottery. My beauty makes me forget the things that always stay the same. Like an uneventful life. Like this dreary town, no airport, a grey place – there's no escape from it and no one ever comes here, no heart-throb, no white knight on his white horse.

Arras. Population 42,000, 4 hypermarkets, 11 supermarkets, 4 fast-food outlets, a few medieval streets, a plaque in the Rue du Miroirde-Venise telling passers-by and anyone who may have forgotten that Eugène-François Vidocq, an early private eye, was born here on 24 July 1775. And then there's my haberdashery shop.

Naked and beautiful in front of the mirror, I feel as if I'd only have to beat my arms in the air and I could fly away, light and graceful. As if my body might join the bodies in the art books lying about my childhood home. And then it would be as beautiful as them. Definitely.

But I never dare try.

The sound of Jo downstairs always takes me by surprise. It tears the silk of my dream. I get dressed again double quick. Shadows cover the clarity of my skin. I know about the wonderful beauty beneath my clothes, but Jo never sees it.

He did once tell me I was beautiful. That was over twenty years ago, when I was little more than twenty. I was wearing a pretty blue dress with a gilt belt, a fake touch of Dior about it; he wanted to sleep with me. He complimented me on my nice clothes.

So you see, we always tell ourselves lies.

Because love would never stand up to the truth.

Jo is Jocelyn. My husband for the last twenty-one years.
He looks like Venantino Venantini, the handsome
actor who played Mickey with the stammer in *The Sucker*
and Pascal the hitman in *Crooks in Clover*. A firm jaw,
piercing eyes, an Italian accent that would have you faint-
ing with pleasure, suntanned skin, dulcet tones that would
give a girl goosebumps, except that my own Jocelyno
Jocelyni weighs ten kilos more than the film star and has

an accent that's a long way from turning a girl's head.

He's been working for Häagen-Dazs since they opened their factory here in 1990. He earns two thousand four hundred euros a month. He dreams of a flat-screen TV instead of our old Radiola set. And a Porsche Cayenne. And a nice fireplace in the living room. A complete set of James Bond films on DVD. A Seiko watch. And a younger, prettier wife, but he doesn't tell me that bit.

We have two children. Well, three, in fact. A boy, a girl and a corpse.

Romain was conceived on the evening when Jo told me I was beautiful, and on account of that lie I lost my head, my clothes and my virginity. There was one chance in thousands that I'd fall pregnant the very first time, and it happened to me. Nadine arrived two years later, and after that I never returned to my ideal weight. I stayed large, a sort of empty pregnant woman, a balloon full of nothing.

An air bubble.

Jo stopped thinking I was beautiful, he stopped touching me. He hung out in front of the Radiola in the evenings, while eating the ice cream they gave him at the factory and drinking Export 33 beers. And I got into the habit of falling asleep on my own.

One night he woke me. He had a hard-on. He was drunk, and he was crying. So I took him inside me, and that night Nadège made her way into my belly and drowned in my flesh and my sorrow. When she came out eight months later she was blue. Her heart was silent. But she had beautiful fingernails and long, long eyelashes, and although I never saw the colour of her eyes, I'm sure she was pretty.

On the day of Nadège's birth, which was also the day of her death, Jo laid off the beers. He broke things in our kitchen. He shouted. He said life was lousy, life was shit, fucking shit. He hit his chest, his forehead, his heart, the walls. He said life was too short. It wasn't fair. You want to rescue what you can from all the shit because time is not on your side. My baby, he added, meaning Nadège, my little girl, where are you? Where are you, poppet? Romain and Nadine were scared and went to their room, and that evening Jo began dreaming of the nice things that would make life sweeter and blunt the pain. A flat-screen TV. A Porsche Cayenne. James Bond. And a pretty woman. He was sad.

My parents called me Jocelyne. There was one chance in millions that I'd marry a Jocelyn, and that one chance came my way. Jocelyn and Jocelyne. Martin and Martine. Louis and Louise. Laurent and Laurence. Raphaël and Raphaëlle. Paul and Paule. Michel, Michèle. One chance in millions.

And it happened to me.

THE FIRST THING YOU SEE
Grégoire Delacourt

A WATERSTONES BOOK CLUB PICK AND INTERNATIONAL BESTSELLER

Imagine you are a young mechanic living in a small community in France. You own your own home, and lead a simple life. Then, one evening, you open your front door to find a distraught Hollywood starlet standing in front of you. This is what happens to Arthur Dreyfuss in the village of Long, population 687 inhabitants.

But although feigning an American accent, this woman is not all that she seems. For her name is Jeanine Foucamprez, and her story is very different from the glamorous life of a star. Arthur is not all he seems, either; a lover of poetry with a darker past than one might imagine, he has learnt to see beauty in the mundane.

The First Thing You See is a warm, witty novel about two fragile souls learning to look beyond the surface – for the first thing you see isn't always what you get!

'This smart romantic comedy is charmingly Gallic and cries out to be filmed as a sentimental comedy' *The Sunday Times*

'At once tender and harrowing, light-hearted and profound, it is a highly original and affecting read' *The Lady*

WE ONLY SAW HAPPINESS
Grégoire Delacourt

There is nothing like the love of a parent for a child. But what happens when that love falters?

Deprived of his parents' love as a child, Antoine is determined to give his son and daughter the perfect childhood he never had. He is a dreamer, an optimist, a man who fell in love at first sight and who believes that he has found the secret to living a happy life.

But when tragedy strikes he becomes someone even he does not recognise. Taken to his lowest point, he performs an act of desperation. But can he find a way back? And what does happiness actually mean?

Provocative, unpredictable, heart-breaking and heart-warming, *We Only Saw Happiness* is a story about families, the choices we make, and the people we become.

'A very moving French story. Delacourt writes with potent simplicity; I didn't want to stop reading' *Evening Standard*